WHAT'S A "RORK"?

Ran Lomar observed the rork in the second before it rose and walked. His first rork!

How large was it, he could not say, having nothing to measure it against but the redwing. Like a great black boulder, it seemed, shading into dark grey below. Spider! Yes, that would have been the obvious comparison, and the term would lead to no confusion since Pia 2 was without arachnids of its own. There was no separate head, and the body was underslung, lower than the knees of the creature's legs, so that it hung—so to speak—from its own thighs, rather than being supported upon them. A daddy longlegs type of animal, with body much larger in proportion to legs than that harmless wee creature of Old Earth, and . . . legs . . . yes. There was no doubt of it. In this respect, at least, the old books were right. The rork was quadruped . . .

RORK!

AVRAM DAVIDSON

A BERKLEY MEDALLION BOOK
published by
BERKLEY PUBLISHING CORPORATION

The author wishes to acknowledge
his debt to Grania Davidson and
Damon Knight for their help in
constructing this book.

BERKLEY MEDALLION EDITION, OCTOBER, 1965

*BERKLEY MEDALLION BOOKS are published by
Berkley Publishing Corporation
15 East 26th Street, New York, N.Y. 10010*

Printed in the United States of America

Rango, the Tame Tock, sweated earnestly at his work in the little valley between Blicky-Got-Caught and Last Ridge. It was farther south than most Tocks cared to work—it was farther south than Rango cared to work, for that matter, but he was inspired by a double ambition. No one else seemed to have visited the valley lately, and it was all aflame with redwing. It was easier to go along just pulling up the plants without straightening up for as long as he could, although he would certainly pay for this later. But his back was bound to ache anyway, and this way he could get more done. A bottle of water and some baked tataplants rested in a shaded hollow, along with a bundle of longgrass. When he felt he could stoop no longer Rango was going to tie up the redwing with the grass. Eat. Rest. When the sun began its long decline, it would be time to leave and get to his housey before sundown and the endless clamor of the nocturnal crybabies marked an end to safety. Tomorrow the redwing, and all the other redwing dumped beside his housey, was going to the Tocky Store at the Guild Station to be turned in for chits. Some of the chits would buy the makings of a big pot of tockyrot and a nice, long drunk. He hadn't had one in a long time, and he needed one.

But the other chits would go, as so many other chits had already gone, to that canny hag, Ista the Lady-doctor. And when, oh, soon there were a hundred of them, Ista was going to make him a charm to go on a long thong around his neck. With it he would be safe, quite safe, this far south and even souther if he dared —safe against rorks.

It was the third generation after the Third War for the Galaxy. Nothing as vivid as "the collapse of civilization" had taken place, but the human race—even that small portion of it in the predominantly nonhuman, and hence noncommitted, so-called "Free Worlds"—the human race was tired. Still tired, after three generations. The ancient Napoleonic Wars were said to have reduced the average height of the French by inches; the Plata Wars of the same century, to have killed off eighty percent of the over-fourteen male population of forgotten Paraguay, which had never recovered. Something lik⸻

had happened here. The cost was too great, in lives and spirit and money and material, to allow for any expansion or extra effort or advance—for anything more, in fact, than a tired and almost failing grip on stasis.

You did the job you had with a minimum of effort, and you stayed with it and were cautious and frugal and saving because your pension was meager. "The Hundred Worlds" had a nice round sound to it, and it was both pedantic and bad form to point out that before the First War the figure had grown to a hundred and thirty-one, and that after the Third War it had dwindled to seventy-four.

Of these, the most remote was Pia 2. Long *i*. You called it *Piatude* if you felt waggish, or *Ptolemy Soter* if you felt formal; that is, if you ever heard of it; but probably you never had.

Edran Lomar had, and of course so had everyone else aboard the Q Ship that put down there every fifth year; but Lomar was probably the only one of them who was glad he had. To the others it was just another dreary run to another dreary colonial outpost. To Lomar it was salvation and dreams come true. At least it had been so. Now, the long voyage from Tranfer Ten (following the long voyage from Old Earth) was beginning to wear away at his assurance.

"You *asked* to go there?" How very, very tired he was of being asked that same question in the same tone of incredulity. Even more tired than he was of the stale, stale air and the heavy, heavy pulsebeat of the ship.

People didn't volunteer to go to Pia 2. Oh, it was no penal colony like Trismegistus, no Hell World. But it was poor and it was remote—not so much in distance, though it was far enough. There were several places much more distant. Thule. Usk. Hyperthule. Conway's Comfort, one side bathed perpetually in the blood-red light of its great and dying sun; the other turned forever like a blind eye toward a dead black sky in which shone never more than three dim tiny stars. Loki. Gorgo. And solitary, solitary Hermes Trismegistus.

But even the farthest of these had its annual transport. To Pia 2 the transport—one, count it, one—came every five years. In this age of least effort and least resistance it had nothing that anybody wanted enough to justify any

6

more frequent connection. Guildsmen didn't *go* there, they were *sent*. And not good Guildsmen, either, for that would be a waste. The fog-heads and the fog-ups. The incompetent and the noncriminal incorrigible. Those who would have been discharged in an earlier, more active age. It wasn't Van Dieman's Land, or the White Man's Grave.

There were similarities, though.

But if you wanted to get away, not just far, far away, but so that whatever was behind you wouldn't and couldn't come crowding on after you, there could hardly (it had seemed to Ran Lomar), there could hardly be a better place.

He'd dreamed of it since he was sixteen. Now, sitting in the Oval, which was the combination library, lounge, quiet-games room, and occasional chapel of the Q, those dreams seemed no longer so vivid and convincing. He tried to ignore the mutterings of the off duty engineer seated nearby who was perpetually trying to perfect (seemingly for his own private satisfaction alone) some mathematical sequences which perpetually defied perfection, tried to ignore the taste-heavy closeness of the re-re- infinitely re-filtered air and the throb, throb, like an aching tooth, of the Q's ancient engines. . . . Since he was sixteen, he'd dreamed, since things . . . not when they first began to get intolerable back on stuffy, rigid, fossilized Old Earth—it seemed that they had always been intolerable—but when he had first realized that it might not be impossible after all to get far, far away from them.

Ran had applied for duty on Pia 2 as early as he could, when he was twenty-one. But his majority had arrived too close to the departure of the next Q Ship. It was full, the people at the posting office had told him, with the curious looks which were to become so common. It was full; he'd have to wait. And so for five years, five fretting, fuming, finger-biting years, he had waited. He didn't care what official duties might be assigned to him, the day on Pia 2 was thirty hours long and the work day only five. Its Station was able to grant frequent long vacations, and there was—and this was it, this was the thing, the whole thing—*there was a whole uncluttered continent to be free in!*

The sudden assignment to a definite duty was thrust

7

upon him at the last moment simply (so they solemnly told him) because he was already on the list and posted for passage in the Q and another man could not be added. It seemed reasonable, though, to assume that it had been given to Ran Lomar, and not any other on the list, because in all probability Ran Lomar was the only one on the list who hadn't fogged up things somewhere else. It was the faintest and most left-handed of compliments. He didn't care about that aspect of it one fig; but the assignment was quite certainly an important one, or seemed to be from the hasty and scanty information supplied him by the Assistant to the Clerk of the Delegate of the Directorate (oh, how they loved titles on Old Earth!—and the longer the better) of the Guild of the Second Academy of Science and Commerce. And this might—probably would—almost certainly would— make everything different. *How* different, Ran could not know. No one on the Q could. No one else on the Q cared, of course. . . .

There was no mystery why his head ached so.

Second Station Aide Aquilas Arlan, looking for Commercial Aide Reldon, found him, finally, in the bar at the Shore Club. No one else would have expected to find him in his office, but a semi-total inability to distinguish the ideal from the actual was probably the reason for Arlan's being on Pia 2.

Reldon gave over caressing his elaborately waxed, long red moustaches and lifted his glass. "Dead rorks," he said.

"Are your records all ready?" Arlan asked, fussily as ever. "The Q is due, you know."

"Have a drink."

"But the Q—"

"Maybe it'll be late."

An expression of astonishment closely approaching horror settled on the Station Aide's face. "The Q is never late. The Q? Late? How can it be late? No, oh, no, it won't be late."

"Have a drink. Here. Dead rorks."

With a nervous little titter Arlan took the drink, glanced automatically around for the censure (it was early, early, early) that was never forthcoming, lifted his glass. "Uh . . . well . . . you'll have your records

8

ready, won't you? Oh! Dead rorks." Titter . . . titter. . . .

"Dead rorks. Boy, bring drinks, quick-quick. Ah. Finish that. Take the other. Dead rorks."

"Dead rorks."

"Dead rorks."

The Mister Flinders of Flinders Crag was angry. He was angry more often than not, every bristle on his face standing out like a quill. At such times only his ancient mother dared call him "Florus." But now he was hungry-angry. His heir-son sat stiff and almost straight, his guests were silent, the picknins hid under the table, and his wife spoke shortly and to the point—both most unusual for her.

"Where in the muck-Hell is eats?" he shouted.

"They none gots the gut to tell," his wife said, her pale underlip trembling very slightly. "But I gots the gut. Eats? So here is eats." She set the bowl heavily on the table. It rattled. "Eat good," she added the ritual words with a resigned bitterness.

The Mister plunged his fist into the bowl, brought it out, opened his fingers. The heavy slugs fell back with a clatter. He glared around the table, dirty with food spots and the drippings of the stinking fish-oil lamps.

"Bullets for breckfus," muttered the old mother. She had witnessed such scenes often enough, and had put the bowl of bullets down herself, times enough. "No eats in the camp. . . . I's to starve, in me age . . . Florus? . . ." Then she lifted up her head and clawed a wisp of dusty hair from her eyes. Her mouth opened, toothless as a lizard's, and she grimaced, shaking her tiny fists. "Be's ya men?" she shrilled. "Be's ya men? Be's ya men? Or be's ya what they calls ya to North? *Tocks! Tocks!* Not men but dirty Tocks!"

The Mister swallowed bitter spit. "Dirty be's as dirty does," he growled. "Guests—me shame. I'll soon pride it." He turned to his heir. "Strip, what's powder?"

"Not much," Strip said.

"Not much, says. Bullets? Alls in the bowl?"

"Most."

For another moment The Mister Flinders growled and mumbled. "Be time for North again, I sees. How I hates it. Time to trade redwing, as gots our blood on it

9

and our dads' and dads' dads' blood. Trade for penny scraps of iron and sulfur. Time for crawl to Guild again. The pogues, the dirty muck-Hell pogues." He slammed his fist on the table and lurched to his feet. Hastily, everyone at the board did the same.

"But none goes North on empty gut!" he shouted. "Hasn't I took Nimmai's muck long enough? Hasn't I waited for that one to pay damage? Is we to gots bullet for breckfus when he gots meat and fish and flour? Hey, say?"

Strip, loudly, said, "No, Dad! Raid! Raid! Raid-raid!" Feet stamped, fists pounded.

Flinders nodded, his grievance against The Mister Nimmai up in red-hot flames again. "That one thinks he safe in Nimmai Camp with his eleven pair o' lock, and one don't fire!" Laughs, sneers, pounding, stamping, shouting. "Haven't Flinders Crag gots twenty pair?" His face redder, his voice hoarser, "Haven't Flinders Crag gots twenty pair, says? *Haven't—*"

He stopped and his voice echoed and his eyes darted down the table-board. A guest, his heavy face set in long grey hair, cleared his throat. "Twenty-seven, host Mister," he said, in phlegmy tone. Another shout, more stamping.

The other guest threw back his head. The noise stopped. The Mister Flinders faced him, more eager than angry. "Crame won't be to walk where Haggar runs," he said, running his grey tongue over his rough lips. "Hey, Crame? Say?"

Said the second guest, "Haggar runs as Haggar wants. Flinders' damage be's Flinders' deal. I be's friend and guest to ya, but ya knows Nimmai nursed at me mumma's dug."

Flinders, scornful, pale with disappointment at the loss of Crame's ten matchlockmen, yet somewhat cautious, hopeful yet: "A dug-brother!"

"Dug-brother better to no brother."

Flinders kicked the trestle. The table shivered but did not fall. He walked to the open door, gazed over the blacklog roofs of Flinders Camp, steaming and smoking in the grey drizzle. Only a short ways away the ground broke and fell off into the long, gaunt escarpment which was its name and its chief defense. Strip came up behind, and to him The Mister said, without turning, "Mus-

10

ter the 'locks. Take a pot of fire, but no matchlights and no powder yet. Maybe the rain s'll break. Haggar! My pride. I'll not shame ya."

Crame made formal thanks and farewell. Flinders waved his hand. Hunger, anger, craft, mingled on his narrow face. "You s'll join me yet, guest-Mister," he said. "If we be's Tocks, be's Wild ones. Same blood. And there be's quicker meat for rorks to eat than weed stalk. *Move!*" he cried, swinging at Strip. *"Raid!"*

The Mister Crame and his men left in silence. Behind them the cry became a chant.

"Raid! Raid! Raid-raid-raid!"

The Q Ship came down, and passengers and crew blinked at the novel sight of men, rather than machinery —long lines of sweaty, dirty, ragged men—loading and unloading. Five years of supplies came ashore, were replaced by packs and packs of strong-smelling, rank-smelling redwing, bound for the distilleries on Hercules to be turned into the medical fixative which was its only use— and the only use of Guild Station/Pia 2—and, therefore, as far as the rest of the Hundred Worlds were concerned, the only, only use of Pia 2 itself.

The Q Ship went up again, not long after—up, up, up, in a crash of sound and a shimmering mist of many colors. The noise seemed to deafen everyone below. They went around with their faces screwed up and couldn't hear anything that was said to them. Of course little was. Of course it wasn't the noise. Not just the *noise* of the takeoff, the physical sound. It was the other noise that echoed in their heads. Five years, five years. Five years. Five years. Five *years*—five *years*—five *years*.

And Edran Lomar, having seen his baggage deposited in the musty, dusty old U-frame building which was to be his, all his, for the next five years (unless he chose to move in with someone or have someone move in with him), found himself in some perplexity as to what to do next.

Second Aide Arlan, who had been "helping" him ("Is that the new regulation compact-unit? Surely you want to change to shore uniform. Your rating is only three but I wouldn't worry, there are going to be vacancies, there always are, and no one coming in to fill them

11

from Outside."), suddenly stopped, blinked, became a good deal more human.

"I was new here once, too," he said. "Forget about reporting in; wait till tomorrow. I can take all this in stride because I know that in five years I'll just step aboard the Q and our house in the retirement colony on Coulter *kappa* is only two trips away. But lots of the others. . . . Never mind. Come home with me, eh? Meet the family. I don't know what the Tockies have got fixed for supper, but it'll be good and ample. Q Day doesn't shake *them* up. Because they're never going anyplace. Eh?"

This grey little fidget of a man, Arlan . . . appearance, manner, everything about him reeked of the conventional, cubed types of which Lomar had had overmuch back home. But at least the man made a kind of sense, provided a sort of raft to cling to for the little while before he would strike out and swim for himself. He accepted the invitation.

"May I ask, Ran," the Second Aide, at home, smiled with the formal informality of his class, "if you are familiar with the Coulter System by any chance?"

"Heigh-ho," sighed his wife, with a studiedly patient shrug of her comfortable shoulders. "Here comes the Tocky with the tray—goody. Take something, cute. You, too, Arlan. Let us eat, drink, and be regulation, for in five years we retire. . . ." She and her husband began to talk to him, more or less at once, and he paid little attention to either and so caught only snatches of talk.

Husband: ". . . retirement colony . . . Coulter *kappa* . . . wonderful climate . . . our kind of people . . . Academy classmates . . . like old times. . . ."

Wife: ". . . Old Earth . . . you'll just die here . . . terrible and colonial and remote . . . terrible long days . . . some Station girl, and before long you won't be able to stand her . . . young enough to interest you means that she grew up here and won't know anything . . . fly the fence . . . Tocky girl . . . tear the shirt off your back. . . ."

Husband: ". . . cheap . . . special prices for pensioned Guildsmen . . . hunting preserves . . . get-togethers . . . lots of fun . . . old times. . . ."

Wife: ". . . read every book on the place . . . want to build a raft and go explore North Cold . . . won't

. . . drinking and playing . . . wonder what you did to wind up here . . . women wearing Outside these days? . . ."

The drinks weren't bad. ("Dead rorks," said the Arlan wife, cheerfully, lifting hers.) The food wasn't bad. In his mind Ran was making plans. Get out on a look-see trip as fast as he could. Locate the source of the salt-smelling air. . . . Wasn't Guild Station situated not far from the Northern Sea? Get far, *far* away from all these niddering voices, crowding bodies. . . . There was an Arlan child present, too—a plain, quiet girl who said nothing. The house was a copy of something thirty years old. He stopped looking, listening awhile. When his mind began registering once again the conversation had shifted to something somewhat more interesting.

The wife: "Of course, our Tocks have been well-trained, but the others . . . well, you'll be visiting Tocky-town, of course. You'll see for yourself. Dirty, filthy, im-*mor*-al, and, oh! bone-lazy."

The husband (comfortably noncensorious): "Well, Linny, they're happy the way they are. I don't blame them. No responsibilities. Umm . . . you don't mind if I tell Ran the old joke?" A titter. "You know what a well-bred Tock is? One who pisses only in the corner of his housey. 'Housey,' that's what they call their huts, you know."

Lomar nodded. There were other groups like that else-where in the Hundred Worlds. There were the Two Tribes on Burnside *beta*. And, off in the Semi-Circle, the Redhaired People of Hercules, the Chickers of New Australia (an ostentatious command of Chicker Cant was a mark of the well-traveled spacer), and the Poor Greens of Humboldt Six.

"The Tocks," he said. "Tockies. Natives of here? Refu-gees from somewhere else? The old books don't mention them. And there are hardly any new books about here . . . unless you count Captain Conybear." He laughed, Linny Arlan laughing with him. Captain Conybear, the Munchausen of the Third Age of Space.

"Oh, yes, Captain Conybear," she said, appreciatively. "How I Fought Off The Wild Tocks. How I Slew The Man-Eating Rork Single-Hand. How I Met The Hermit Of Hollow Rock."

The SA, evidently not approving of the very nonregu-

13

lation Captain Conybear, made a noise which might have been agreement, disagreement, a chuckle, or a grunt. "Might call them natives, although they didn't start out that way. Refugees, hmm, sort of. Oh, you haven't had the chance to see any General Orders yet, have you? *Officers, Men, and Autochthonous Persons.* That's them. Autochthonous, Tocks, Tockies. Well, they're the descendants of the original settlers before, oh, way before the First War. You don't know what happened then? The war lasted sixty years. You do know that. And for forty years no ship put down here. Not one ship. They were on their own. And they didn't make it. No . . . they didn't make it. . . .

"Because even after that first ship did come, it was a long time, damned long, before any other one came. And after that, even, it was a long time before the ships started coming regularly and Guild Station was reestablished."

They were on their own. And they didn't make it.

Ships had come often in the days of the original settlement. No one then had thought in terms of self-sufficiency. And then, suddenly, they stopped coming—not just often, but at all. There had been two more wars since then, interrupting communications. The settlers (who hadn't originally thought of themselves as settlers, any more than the present off-planet personnel of Guild Station did) had had to scrabble. It had been root, hog, or die. Many had died. Education, culture, social ways, science, and marriage, had crumbled and vanished. The local Tocks no longer had husbands, wives, or family names.

Or much of anything else, it seemed.

Lomar said, "No wonder they're wild. I thought that Captain Conybear had made that part up."

"What? No, no, these are all Tame Tocks up here. The others, the Wild ones, they live down at the South end of the continent. You'll see them up here, though, when they come to trade. For my part, the less I see of them, the better. Bad numbers. They're killing themselves off, though, and if it weren't for the redwing they bring in, I'd say the sooner the better," he tittered. He began to ramble. "It'll be soon enough, after my time, though, that's all I care about. Less and less redwing comes in every year. Medical fixitive, you know, that's what they use it for; so, do people need less medicine Outside or

14

have they developed a synthetic or found something else? It'll last my time, though, I'll be safe and happy on the games course there on Coulter *kappa* and then let the Wild Tocks kill themselves all off with their homemade popguns. . . ."

Titter.

The decline in redwing production was fairly recent. Until the last decade the amount had scarcely varied from year to year. It was the fault of the Tocks. They were the ones who went out and gathered it. The Wild Tocks trading it for scrap metal and sulphur, made crude guns and cruder gunpowder. The Tame Tocks weren't interested in that, never had been (no, Arlan didn't know when or why the original stock had split into two groups) —food and booze was all they cared for. And, of course, titter, sex. But they didn't have to trade redwing for that. Regulations didn't allow the Station to give them booze. But they could trade for the makings. *Tockyrot,* the stuff was called. Vile stuff. . . .

But that's the way they were. Give them a gut full and a skin full and a (heh heh hee) something else full, and they were happy. Lazy? It was just incredible how lazy they were. Wouldn't work unless they absolutely had to, rather just lie in the sun. Or run around feuding . . . the Wild ones, that is. How many Tocks were there? No one counted. There did seem to be fewer than there used to be.

Presently talk slowed down, ran out. The Arlan girl had excused herself and left, the Arlan wife had fallen into frank slumber. The SA cleared his throat. "It's still early," he said. "I suppose it might be just as well to make a courtesy call at the Residence." The Second Station Aide had obviously made a mental flip through of the Regulations and come to a conclusion.

Lomar felt not the slightest degree of anticipation at the thought. "Ah . . . you don't think . . . tomorrow?"

"Oh, no. Come along. Not a formal reporting in, just a visit. These quintennials take a lot out of the Old Man. He feels the letdown, he'll be glad to see us. Come along."

Servants snapped-to, bowed, saluted, rang gongs, trotted on ahead. The Residency was cool, spic-and-spotless, though crammed with furniture and pictures and

15

cabinets of bric-a-brac. They came at last into a room with hidden lights. A servant was holding a uniform and the man who had just removed it stood beside him. For a moment more the man's figure retained the molded outlines of formality. Then it seemed to sag and melt, found refuge in the quickly offered, quickly donned brocaded wraparound, and sank into an easy chair.

"Aquilas! And a new person!" The voice was rich and mellow, eager, but with overtones of petulance and self-pity. "Oh, these ghastly Q Days! The strain, the strain . . ." The man squinted, slightly frowned. Then a smile distended his rather full, rather loose mouth. "Who is this you've brought along with you to divert my aching nerves? A drinky—we must all have a drinky. Boy, bring drink, quick-quick." The wraparound drooped a bit, revealing his heavy, hairy breasts. Three Tock house-boys, well-fed and coarsely handsome, glanced at Lomar out of the corners of their eyes, hastily glanced away, set to work at the lavish bar.

The Second Station Aide was once again all stiff and starchy. "Sir. I have the honor to present Edran Lomar, newly come aboard, with a rating of three, and not yet reported in. Three Lomar, this is His Respect, the Station Officer, Tan Carlo Harb."

Tan Carlo Harb jiggled in his chair with pleasure. "Not yet reported in! Then we can dispense with formality for the present; good. My dear boy! Let me take your hands. A fresh face—you can have no idea—Hark! Did I hear the sunset gun?" He giggled, helped himself from the tray of glasses, waggled his fingers at his guests to do the same. "Pardon the classical allusion. I know the classics are not popular nowadays. . . . 'Nowadays'—what do we here know of 'Nowadays,' isolated as we are on the very edge of empire, the staff about to fall from our nerveless, bloodless hands? Metaphorically speaking.

"I hope you like the drinky, new face. My boys make good ones. Feckless, swinish lot, these Tocks, one has to observe them every little minute; although as to my own boys, their loyalty is beyond question, as it damned well ought to be, all that I have done for them."

His large, olive-colored eyes traveled Lomar up and down, taking in the whole slender figure from the unfashionably short brown hair and heavy eyebrows, the

16

critical mouth and dissatisfied set of the chin, the rangy limbs to the almost defiantly non-regulation footgear. "Since you are not here, yet, officially," the Station Officer said, "let us—if you will excuse my language while you still have to—cut the crap. What is a decent, alert-looking boy like you doing out here in the absolute ass-end of bloody nowhere?"

Lomar smiled an unprompted, ungrudged smile. No one had asked him to, but nonetheless he felt that he rather liked Tan Carlo Harb. Out with it, then. And then perhaps smile no more. "You will find, sir," he said, "in the official documents I hand over tomorrow when I report in, that although my regular rating is three, I am commanded by Their Serenities the Guild Directorate to function here under an assimilated rating of seven. My assigned duty is to investigate the decline in red-wing production, and use all permissible means to increase that production."

He felt, did not see, the Station Aide stiffen with absolute astonishment beside him. He saw the full, full face of the SO lengthen with what was certainly surprise and might have been dismay as well. The olive eyes were large and blank. Plump, hairy fingers crept around the glass, lifted it. Automatically or otherwise, Tan Carlo Harb announced the traditional toast.

"Dead rorks," he whispered. "Dead rorks . . ."

CHAPTER TWO

REDWING: (also called *Musk-apple, Musk-dragon, Rorks-dinner,* and *Redweed.*) The stalk, which is not gathered, is said to—

Lomar tossed aside the worn copy of Harrel's *Commercial Pharmacopeia of the Outer Worlds.* Thirty-fifth revision of the 20th edition, it had already been theoretically superseded, but the up-to-date versions for this entry which he had looked at on Old Earth had been worded just the same. Obviously the Guild of the Second Academy of Science, Commerce, and the Arts had not come up with a substitute or synthetic; obviously the need for the derivative was still urgent—as urgent as anything ever was in these tired times of Don't Rock The Boat and If You Don't See It It isn't There— or they would not have upped him to a temporary rating of seven and saddled him with the job of increasing production.

Not only did the fact that he had five uninterruptible years sap any sense of urgency he might have had; or the fact that Pia 2 took thirty hours in its circuit around Pia Sol make a siesta a physical, rather than merely a social, necessity; but the whole atmosphere of the place was death to speed and efficiency. He kept telling himself that there was a mostly empty continent about the size of New Zealand waiting for him to go and see. But he still hadn't gone.

He found himself no more able to concentrate here on his own bed than at the old-model desk in his office. All sorts of odd things kept running through his mind. *Officers, Men, and Autochthonous Persons*, for instance. The first, more than mere men, presumably; the latter, less. And how long had it been since there was more than one "officer" here on Pia 2? And what a one he was, too! Not that Ran Lomar liked Tan Carlo Harb much the less for it. It was easy enough to avoid his unspoken invitation. Had the SO been stationed . . . exiled . . . here on Pia 2 because of this peculiarity? Or had it been submerged, only rising to the surface here; or the surface wearing away like greasepaint in the isolation which was life out here? Whichever it was, the Old Man had adjusted, was happy, didn't pull rank to make conquests. Lomar had known of worse SOs by far.

Officers, Men, and Autochthonous Persons. A stupid phrase, typical officialese gobbledygook, frozen here like so much else. *Tocks. Tockies.* An offensive term, particularly when used as distinct from *Men*—and yet they themselves accepted it. The crone who cleaned his U for him, for instance—"Thace two Tocks and a man to see you," so she'd said that morning. It had been old "Cap" Conders, come to show him a fresh batch of redwing start its slow way through the curing sheds he supervised. Big Tock and Shorty, they'd said their names were. Inquiries as to their real names had brought only surprised looks and rotten-toothed grins.

Redwing. The leaf did somewhat resemble a wing. It

18

was as long and as broad as his back, with a long and pulpy stalk which Big Tock had chunked off with his hack then and there. The leaf was still a vivid red somewhere between scarlet and crimson. "I made them get you a nice prime one, still fresh, so you could see, yes," said the old man. "Leave it to them, they'll just as soon leave it lie around till it gets shrinky and starts browning, yes. There you are, Brother Ran. That's what we're all here for, yes. That and to protect these poor piss-ants from the rorks. If it weren't for us the rorks would soon overrun the place and scour it clean, yes. Oh, good-morning! Haven't I shot enough of them in my time—haven't I, you, Big Tock?"

And Big Tock, looking up from his grey toes wiggling in the dirt: "Oh, yace, Mist Cap. Oh, yace."

Lomar protested. "What for, Cap? I mean, why shoot them? Aren't they harmless unless you attack them first?"

There was no make-believe in the bloodshot eyes at all. "You'll learn different," the old man said. "You aren't the first who came here believing everything he read in some book three hundred years old, yes. You ask these boys—they know—they'll tell you. Tell him about the rorks, Big Tock. Go on."

Big Tock stopped scratching a naked armpit whose skin showed slightly white against the general grime. He shivered, spat three times, dipped his big toe in the puddly craters. "Oh, yace," he said, his voice lower. "We s'll all be dead, all, if the men don't protex us fro the spiders—"

"Spiders?"

"That's their name for the rorks. Go on, Big Tock, tell him about when you were a boy—"

"Yace, Mist Cap. When I a boy, wece livin in a housey too far fro Tockeytown. Me mumma's fella go fro brower ("Brower?" "Borrow, he means.")—goce brower fire, becus why, becus fire goce out in housey. He hafs to go too far. My mumma gahst two-three lilla baby. Ist come nigh-time. Inna nigh-time we mussa falla sleep. Becus me mumma's fella goce back wista fire, one lilla baby we cahn fine im. Becus alla crybaby they crine too. And we cahn tell witsta crybaby an witsta real baby. . . ."

Big Tock told his story so far matter-of-factly enough, but Lomar winced. He could, suddenly, picture the di-

19

lemma. How *would* you be able to locate a crying baby, a human child, with the trees and bushes and shrubs and grass full of the little insectivorous woods creatures whose cry for all the world was that of a wailing infant?

"Becus real lilla baby he jus learnin walk. Inna nightime when wece sleepin he mussa walkin outa housey. An we loosk and we loosk and we yellin. Nen we *hear* —*Ukh*—!"

A rictus of fear convulsed his face. Shorty shivered. Conders looked at Lomar, who asked, "Hear *what?*"

"Hear *spider*. Too near. Goce, *'Rork! Rork!'* An wece knowin ista spider becus wece hearin him rorkin. Nen wece runnin back to housey anna nex day we loosk again an we seece lilla blood here an lilla blood there. But we never fine lilla baby. Spider take im for eats im. Yace."

There was a moment's silence. Lomar felt his flesh prickling. It hardly seemed a fairy tale he'd just heard. Conders said, as casually as if he had been discussing the morning menu, or as if the two of them had been quite alone, "Well, that's the Tocks for you. Running off just like that and leaving a baby at the mercy of the rorks. Dirty, cowardly, piss-poor worthless people, that's what they are. Of course, the girls, yes . . . ."

Conders snickered. "You'll be changing your luck with one of these Tocky girls, soon, I guess," he said. "They're hot stuff, all right. All the young men have them, yes. They'll tumble for money, marbles, chalk, or just for fun. Oh, I know it—good morning! I must've tumbled hundreds of 'em. And I'm not all worn out yet, either." His reddish eyes rolled around towards Lomar, as if in challenge; his cracked lips leered.

Lomar was not presently interested in the thought of taking a tumble with a female equivalent of Shorty or Big Tock. Of course, the idea held a certain academic interest, wasn't to be forever rejected out of hand. Loving —if it was good loving—soaked in. But it didn't last forever.

Reluctantly, now, on the bed in his upstairs room in the U (plenty of room here at Guild Station, where the buildings had been set up in more populous times), he turned his thoughts to other, local and immediate thoughts. His mind returned now to the comment of the

20

Station Aide, Arlan, about finding a substitute for or a synthetic form of the redwing derivative . . . that curious substance which had the power to force more subtle medicinal substances to stay bonded and not go flying off to join the universal ether . . . it had not been a very realistic comment. Arlan was just making conversation.

When were discoveries in any field made nowadays? Never . . . or next to never. Nobody did anything new, nobody ever tried. Nobody rocked the boat, went looking for trouble. Everybody just held on because nobody dared let go. Maybe if they did it wouldn't take them as long as it had the Tame Tocks to become the way they now were.

The Tame Tocks . . . marooned here forever in their thin strip of territory on the top of the continent. Listlessly going through the outback parts of North Tockland, pulling up redwing, dragging the bundles of it back to their stinking hovels, hacking off the stalks, turning in the leaves for Guild chits which enabled them to buy the cast-off clothes and the coarser foodstuffs at the Station store reserved for them. Scratching about and growing scant patches of crops. Acting as the cheapest kind of cheap labor for Station and its personnel. Mixing their pot-batches of tockyrot and hardly waiting for it to become fully fermented before guzzling it. Big drunks, fights, orgiastic matings. Lying around for days, sleeping it off. Whoring. Dozing in the sun. "Sick. Yace. Sick. Cahn work t'day. Sick."

His job seemed doomed before he could get it started.

Standing on the flats of yellowgrass behind the curing sheds, the heavy rank musty odor now and then blown away by the tempting salt-sea wind, Lomar had made his first attempt.

"Look here . . . Why don't you bring in bigger loads of weed, you Tocks?"

"Cahn carry im, Mist Ran. Too heavy."

"Yes, but look here. You see a stand of redwing. You tear it up by the roots. You make up your load. You drag it in. Then you hack off the roots, the stalks. Then you sell the leaf. Now—don't you see? If you hacked off the roots and stalks as soon as you pulled the plant up, you'd be able to make up loads that wouldn't be any heavier but would be all leaf."

21

Blank stares. Scratching of rumps. "You see . . . half your labor, maybe more, goes into dragging along the roots and stalks, the part of the plant that's of no use to us. Why bother? If you do it my way, you bring in a load that's a hundred percent salable. You don't have to do any more work, but you can get more money. . . . Don't you see?"

They did not see. This is the way things were done. Things were done this way. Things weren't done another way. You did things the way you did things. You didn't do things the way you didn't do things. Thus, the Tocks. But—

But did you really need the Tocks?

The Commercial Aide sat in his office looking steadily at a bottle set in the absolute middle of the table. The morning was only half over. He had spent an hour in front of his mirror, putting his red moustaches into their elaborate convolutions with the thick and gummy stuff called "Chicker spit." He looked up slowly from the bottle as Lomar entered. A wide and rather shyly charming smile began to spread slowly over his long, pale face.

"Reldon! I—"

"See what the dice-devils have sent me for a present," Reldon said. "Have a drink." He pressed his palms flat to the tabletop, but Lomar motioned him not to rise.

"Reldon, I came here to tell you—"

"Tell me over a drink. It will sound much better, believe me." A single 3D picture hung askew on the light brown wall. Young men in uniform. Reldon's class at the Academy. It was covered with dust. Aside from this the room was bare of the usual clutter—family portraits, scenic views, souvenirs, record scans, record spools. Just the bottle on the desk.

"Thanks, thanks, it's too early for me to drink, and besides something has just occurred to me that may be the answer to—"

Reldon's smile faded, trembled. "It's not too early for *me* to drink. Not if I've got a legitimate reason to. It *is* too early for me to be drinking by myself. That, I've got to watch. But, oh, no harm surely in a social drink? Hey? *Sure*. Hey?" His pale hands with their prominent blue veins twitched as he talked. Lomar's face indicated reluctant consent and Reldon jumped up, jerking open a

22

wall file marked *Urgent* so suddenly that the glasses in it clattered together.

"Dead rorks!" said Reldon, cheerfully. He splashed himself another, questioned Lomar with eyes and eyebrows, shrugged at the refusal. Drank again— "Dead rorks . . ."

"What is this thing that everyone has about rorks?" Lomar sipped cautiously. Whatever was in the glass had not been mixed with anything lighter, was strong.

Reldon grimaced. "You've never seen one."

"Have you?"

Nodding over his glass, Reldon took away his lips. "Yes. Horrible things. Finish your drink. Another."

But Ran wouldn't. "No, I want to tell you about my idea. . . ." It came tumbling out of him . . . Tocks . . . wasteful labor . . . wasted time . . . impossible to get them to make even the simplest changes. . . .

"But look. Do we need the Tocks? Do we really *need* them?"

Reldon squinted, unaccustomed thought coming hard and painful. "Well, who in the Hell else is going to gather that stinking muskweed?"

Eyes bright, lips eager, Lomar put his hands on the other man's shoulders. "Grow it!" There. It was out. "Plant it and grow it! It's been done, did you know that? Only experimentally, but it's been *done*. It's in the old books. Before the First War broke out, over five square kilometers were planted into redwing. Did you know that?"

"Mmm. No. Didn't. Finish your—"

But Lomar wanted him to catch fire, too. Didn't he see? Didn't Reldon understand? The Guild wanted redwing production increased, and this was the way to do it. True, there was no agricultural equipment on hand—*but it could be made!*"

" 'Made'?" Reldon had perhaps never heard the verb. "How—'made'?"

"Improvised. It can be improvised. The skimmers, for ex—"

Skimmers. Whatever vague emotion that had passed for interest now ebbed quite out of Reldon's face. Skimmers. Not his pidgin. The Motor Aide should be the one to see. Starchy Manton, the one who had the crazy notion that he was always in danger of being lured onto

23

the Q and killed or shanghaied or something . . . See him. Nothing to do with Reldon, skimmers—

"Nothing to *do* with you—? Hell! You're the Commercial Aide. Has this place got any other commerce besides redwing? The Directorate's orders are that redwing production be increased. And—"

Reldon's long, pale fingers, trembling only the slightest now that three drinks had restored his equilibrium, caressed the elaborate whorls of his moustaches. He seemed to draw confidence from their stiff contours. "Well, you see, my boy. The Guild. The Directorate. Their orders. Mmm. Well, yes. But you forget. Those orders are addressed to you. They aren't addressed to me. I don't care. I don't have to care. All I have to do is keep the records. Which I do. Oh, I get behind. Lots and lots, I get behind. But I catch up in time for the Q.

"You're enthusiastic. That's not usual. That's very much not usual. People today are not enthusiastic. They used to be. What did it get us. Three galactic wars. I'm ten, twelve years your senior. And the only things which ever make me even the least bit enthusiastic are this—" he touched the bottle "—and, sometimes," he touched his fly, "—this. But mostly just *this*. There's nothing here or there's nothing there and there's nothing anywhere else that's worth really getting bothered about. So . . . mmm . . . so . . ." He looked blankly at Lomar, blinked. Wet his lips. Moved his hands. Then a thought came to him, perhaps not the one which had just escaped his mind, but a welcome one nonetheless. "Finish your drink," he urged. "Hey? Another. . . . Dead rorks!"

The long motor shed in which the Station's twenty skimmers were kept had room for twenty hundred. It was obvious that even the ones on hand were scarcely used. What for? Inspecting? Exploring? Who had any interest in either. Ten of the vehicles, packed in protective, were up on racks. Five of them were being stripped down as Lomar, fuming and fretting, stalked in.

The Tock grease monkeys were slowly cleaning them off under the cold, fixed eye of the Motor Aide in the starched armor-stiff uniform that had given him his nickname. Another five skimmers stood, glistening and sharply clean, at the ready. One of these seemed to exude the sweet, spicy scent of whatever it was that the Station Officer used on his well-fleshed, well-kept body. Sure enough, his small banneret hung at the fantail.

The departure of the Q seemed to have abated something of Manton's obsessive preoccupation. He no longer went around (or, as often, stood still) muttering, *First it'll be, Have a drink . . . then it'll be, Come aboard and look around . . . and then—noooo—nooo.* . . . . He actually turned his head as Lomar entered, though only slightly. In a few months he would be relaxed enough to smile. It had only happened once in history that a Q Ship, once gone up, had returned. But not until the mere possibility had gone away would Manton begin to feel safe. Day by day and month by month he would become less obsessed . . . until the hands of the five-yearly clock swung past the half-way mark once more . . . and then, month by month and day by day he would sink beneath the weight of his fears again. No one knew what Q Days cost him, no one could do more than guess. Nor could any do more than conjecture whom it was he suspected of trying to lure him on board, or for what frightful end.

His eyes dismissed Lomar as an immediate danger, rolled back to observe the cleaners at work on the machinery. His body had not relaxed its stiffness sufficiently to wrinkle the rigidly starched uniform so inappropriate for the shed. He listened without expression to Lomar's now less freely flowing plans. Without expression. Without comment.

Impatient, annoyed, but by no means without pity, Lomar asked after a short while, "Well, what do you say?"

Wait. Then, "About what?"

"About *what?* About using the skimmers for plowing and planting and tending and harvesting. Redwing. All we'd need are simple attachments that can be made here. Set the skimmers low enough, a few inches, a few feet—we can figure out the details as we go along—learning by doing—then we won't need to be dependent on the Tockies, don't you see. We can set our own production schedules, and. . . . Well, what do you *say?*"

Manton said, "No."

Lomar felt a slight, very slight recurrence of the start of the dreadful headache which had all but knocked him out those last few hours on the Q Ship. A nerve began to throb painfully. He felt his face grow hot. "Why *not?*" he demanded.

"It's not my job. I have nothing to do with redwing."

Lomar shouted. The tocks, faces smeared with sweat and greasy preservative, looked up. Nothing to do with *redwing?*—Ran shouted. When they all, every single person, had nothing to do with anything *but* redwing? Did Manton suppose that he was stationed here on this nothing place just to gum skimmers up and then clean them off again? Over and over and over again?

Manton said, "No . . . We have one aerospacecraft and one watercraft and I'm responsible for them, too."

"But they're not ends in themselves!—are they?"

The starched man nodded. "As far as I'm concerned. They've got to last us twenty years. Anything breaks down, wrecks—anything—no replacements. Can't take chances. No."

"You're saving them. What are you saving them *for?*"

A shrug. "Not my business. Maybe an emergency. . . . My job is to keep them in shape. Not my job to risk them, use them for something they've never been used for before. Grow redwing. Never heard of a thing like that. Can't use skimmers like that. That's not the way we do things. No."

No.

No.

No.

"My dear boy." The Station Officer chuckled. Looked, smiling, at Lomar, obviously expecting him to chuckle or at least smile in return. The courtesy was not forthcoming. The full face grew a trifle bleak, then relaxed into its habitual amity. Words were lacking, paws waved, throat was cleared. "You are asking me to do what I've never done before. No one has ever done it before."

"But it can be done—it *was* done once, raising redwing as a crop, before the First War—"

No no no. Tut. Not what the SO meant. Not what he meant at *all.* "Upsetting things," he said, vaguely, still gesturing. "Interfering. Charging around and changing things around. We don't operate in that officious and tyrannical manner here. Pulling *rank?* I don't pull rank. Never. Not even a teensy bit. Why, I don't have to. Ev-

26

eryone knows what his job is. No one has to interfere. Reldon's job is commerce. He does it. *Drinks* too much, oh, I grant you," chuckle, "but we are liberal here. The flesh has its demands, you can't put them in fetters of iron. *No*. Point is, he does his *job*. Whatever it is. Manton, poor dear funny fellow, he has *his* job. Motors. Keeps them all in tip-top shapey. I want my skimmer—'Manton. My skimmer.' Zippetty-ping, here it is. Not a speck on it. *Well* . . . Now, I can't go horsing over and interrupting and upsetting things . . . now, *can* I? Nooo. Of course I can't. Same at the Residence. I don't go into the kitchen, tell my Tocky boys, Fry this that way, braise that this way. *They* know what they have to do. They do it. They'd do an-y-thing for me, yes they would, cute: they'd die for me, they'd just die. *'Die!'* that's all I'd have to say, and they'd—"

"Sir—"

"—roll over and drop dead—"

"Sir!"

"You. Edran Lomar. Are raising. Your *voice*. Oh, yes, you are. I am broadminded. I am tolerant. Someone's wife once came into my office without so much as an in-*vita*tion and do you know what she *did*? *She* got down on her silly skinny knees and she *prayed* for me! Oh, I tell you, I did not know where to *look!* But I let her. Yes in-deedy. But there are limits. A simulated or assimilated rating of seven you may have. But I don't wish to remind you. I am not a rating. It isn't my way to refresh your awareness with the fact that I am an officer. But please, cute, please do not raise your *voice* to me. It is so coarse, don't you see, doing that.

"Now, what you *can* do—" Tan Carlo Harb raised his eyebrows and patted his lower lip with the tip of his fat, flat tongue. "I am *al*ways willing to *lis*ten. Come to the Residency tonight. We will dine, we will drink, we will have liqueurs and all the latest fashionable goodies that they've sent me just bundles and *bales* of on the Q. No one will disturb us. The Tockies, those scamps, will clear off and clear out and leave us oh quite alone. And you will talk. And I will listen."

He rose, smiling and rosy and bland and he patted Lomar's shoulders and he put his arm around his waist and he walked him to the door. "Tonight, then, at ten?" he inquired.

27

"Tonight, then, at ten," Lomar agreed, dispirited. The talking and listening, he was quite sure, would get him nowhere. The SO would almost certainly want to wrestle afterwards. And the way Lomar was feeling, he might not even bother to wrestle back.

Outside, in the wide street bordered with the huge taranth-trees which here seemed to attain a luxury of growth greater than on their native world, an old Tocky went by, a can on his head, his voice plaintive and faltering, peddling sea-quirks. Flowering *pi*-vines wound around the old trees, their fronds releasing tiny clouds of purple pollen when the breeze quickened and shook them. Station wives ambled along chatting to each other, servants behind them with baskets of wild and domestic produce sold in the open lot called "the market" by those Tocks lacking the inclination or the energy to hawk their goods through the long and quiet streets. Men in uniform were not lacking—so light were their duties that any excuse sufficed for a break or a visit to another's post.

The daughter of Second Station Aide Arlan came down the street now and stopped in front of him and smiled at him.

This was perhaps the second or third time they had met since the night he had dined with her parents. So different was she at their second meeting, it was as if the girl on that initial evening at her home was only a blurred two-dimensional, black-and-white photograph. What had caused her to withdraw into the inner chamber of her cell that first night, he had not yet learned.

"Hello, Lindel," he said.

There was nothing special about the girl, and yet he had never seen anything quite like her. A phrase, The Wild Colonial Girl, shot through his mind. She wasn't really wild, of course, the way a feral beast was wild. There was something in and about her, though, that couldn't exist on a planet with a traffic problem. A tunic blouse which might have been a tenth copy of a five-year-old pattern from Outside (the new ones as yet wouldn't have had time to burst into transplanted bloom), though new enough to look still little worn, was tucked into a pair of field breeches modeled after the ones men wore, but obviously tailor-made to fit hips and haunches and a fetching little rump.

"Hi, Ran," she said, taking his hand. They fell into step

28

and she still held it. He had been grasped in more intimate places with less surprise . . . but the surprise quickly settled before a more intuitive understanding. She could have been no more than a child when she first came here, so it was natural enough for her to walk hand in hand with any man she met . . . and she had just kept on doing so. It wasn't the custom Outside. No one ever said not to, or indeed ever spoke or even thought about it. But no one ever did it.

"Hi, Ran," she said again, giving their joined hands a firm swing, and looking up into his face. A smile was there for him, her look seemed to say, but it must be earned. His smile came rather rustily, but it came nonetheless. She nodded, she smiled back. There were hints of her mother in her—little of her father but the eyes.

Lomar as yet did not love her in the full sense, but she was so new, so novel, so enchantingly fresh, she had the spice of youth still unstifled, that he was utterly attracted to her. And so, of course, he had already begun to love her, even if just a little bit.

The shore path paused at the top of a bluff. "So— that's the Northern Sea," he said. It was green, and frothy white in regular patterns as far as he could see, not with wind alone (he learned by and by) but from microscopic marine life form as well. The sea stretched on without an end.

"Yes," Lindel said. She pointed far off, low down the horizon. "That's North Cold."

"What? Where? That smudge? Really?"

She laughed. "No, it's a lie. Newcomers always get told that. North Cold, you can never see it from here. Those are just clouds. I think my father said you're a three with a seven rating. That's surely unusual. You know what, Ran? ("What?") If you bring this job off—more redwing —you can skip four ratings. Yes, you can. The Directorate would do it, I bet. Make you a regular seven. Then you could pension out in fifteen years. If you wanted to. Look—"

She stooped, scooped. "—a sea-quirk. Old Daddy Toey must've dropped it out of his basket." She squeezed it and it opened something which might have been a mouth and it went *quirk quiiirk queeerrrkkk* and then closed up again.

29

"We'll have it with our supper. . . ." She tugged at his hand. To the left he could see the beach club at no great distance, bath-house, dance house, games grounds; she tugged him to the right. The path dipped into a hollow, the sea vanished from sight, but not from scent. The sun-warm dust of the path, and the dusty plants it wound between, each had their own distinctive scents . . . dry, warm, sharp, good. . . . Suddenly she stopped. "If you don't want to swim bare we can go to the club," she said. "Some people don't want to. They've got warts or something, you know. . . ."

He spoke to the question in her voice. Only a few very small and inconspicuous warts were all he had, he said. She nodded in a grave, believing fashion which caught at his heart a bit, and his heart said, Go slow, Go easy, You don't know what you really have here, You're here for five more years and so is she, She's so young, Don't go leaping at her or on her. Not just yet, anyway. Not just yet . . .

He'd had better swims and known better swimming spots than that one on the Northern Sea. The bottom was rough where it wasn't mucky-slimy, and the froth (for all the fun they had tossing handfuls of it at each other and posing with it here or there in mock modesty) was unpleasantly sticky stuff, not responding to plunges. In the end it was necessary to scrape it off with sand, and this left them both messy. Too, the high salt context of the quick-drying water left itchy scurfy patches on their skin.

"Well, that's the admission charge," Lindel said, watching him fiddling and plucking. "I hope you weren't hoping very much to make love to me here."

He said, "Well, I was, in a way."

"It's no fun when you're like this. Later, when we're clean, if we want to. What do you think of my body?"

"It's a good body. Be better in a few years. But it's nice, I mean, right now. I hope to get to know it very well."

She nodded, tossed her foam-flecked hair. "Your's is good, too. *I* hope . . . Do you think you'd get tired of it in less than a year? My body, I mean."

"My life, *no*. Less than a *year*?" What could she mean? Nothing was measured in mere years, here. The pulse of the Station had a five-year beat. Lustrum, lustrum . . .

A sort of spark flashed through his mind. "Oh. Who—?"

Her lips moved before she spoke. "Mantosen. My lover. He never would acknowledge me. Oh, everybody knew. But he never danced with me the first or stayed overnight, or let *me* stay overnight or wore my ring, or anything. It was too near to Q time. He was afraid—he said so—he'd be pressured, asked to marry me, because his old meadowmate died, you see, there'd be room for me on the Q. *Pressured!* How much pressure—" Scornfully, she left the phrase unfinished. "I was just a stopgap. I had a gap and he stopped it. And I was, oh, I was so meek and mild and sweet and soft. Oh, I was so *sure!* That he'd change his mind, you know, at the last minute. I was all packed!" Her eyes gleamed, her breath was quick.

But it didn't need Mantosen's failure to tell her it was all no use. She knew that, finally, in enough time. "Oh, what I felt like—and what I felt like doing. I was all burning one minute, all freezing the next. And I made plans in my mind. I'd drug him and hire some Tocks and we'd carry him out, tied up, way out past Last Ridge, and stake him down. And I'd sit in the niche, all safe, you've got to know just where it is, and I'd wait and I'd listen while the rorks came, listen to him scream and scream and *scream*—"

Her voice stopped with a sick sort of jerk. She gazed at him, brimming, resentment covering anything male. And then she cleared her throat. They were dry enough by then to dress; they dressed in silence. No, for sure, for sure, there was nothing like Lindel on Old Earth. There might be on other colonial, scantily peopled worlds, but Lomar wouldn't know.

Back in his U they showered and scrubbed. No trace of past sorrows or hates on her face now, she came unsummoned to his arms. But not undesired, oh no, not undesired. Afterwards she idled with her fingers in the sweat-slicked hairs on his chest and belly, and she sang old Tocky songs in a clear, untrained but sweet voice. They showered again, and while he was dressing she left him and the house without a single word or backward glance.

The SO must have known. It may have been swift gossip, or he may have known just by Lomar's lessened tension or by any one of a half-score of ways of knowing, but Tan Carlo Harb made no fluty suggestions, by word or eye or hand. He was a good host with a good table and a good bar. His house was full of interesting things, his conversation—ranging from the Third Canto of the Galactiad to hunting trips with the Wild Tocks—was easy and entertaining. By the time they set to talk of the major business of the evening Lomar had no desire to raise his voice again.

"Why do you think redwing production has slipped so much these last ten years?" he asked.

Harb pursed his lips, raised his brows, dropped a pinch of pnath into his drink, watched the powder—made from a Lichenoid that grew on the trees of Island L'Vong in the P'Vong Cluster, far off in the Lace Pattern—swell and dance about and then lie still; drank and smacked his lips. "It's the Tocks, my boy. *Why* the Tocks? Ahah . . . For one thing, they have *never* recovered, they have never re*covered* from their years alone. Hundreds of years ago: truuue . . . but . . . oh . . . something happened to them, then. Something went out of them that's never been put back in. Oh, it's easy to say, everybody says it, 'The Tocks are lazy.' I grant you that. I might as well grant you the specific gravity of—oh anything you care to mention. It's a fact. But *why* is it a fact?

"The Tocks no longer *care*. They have slipped so far that they can't get up again. Moral, physical, emotional degeneration. It's self-augmenting. Won't eat properly. Can't live on tockyrot alone, *you* know it, *I* know it. Do *they* know it? If they do, they don't care. Result, my boy? What's the result? A prey to every disease. Or maybe it's all one disease, I don't know— 'Tock fever,' they call it here. No pride, no energy," he said, lolling back in his chair and squinting up at the fresco of naked boys on the near wall of the room. "Inbred, disgustingly so. I wish I had the authority to make every Guildsman who sets foot here throw away his null-fer pills—get some fresh *blood* into the Tocks. . . ."

But he hadn't the authority. Policy was policy. One took the pill as habitually as brushing one's teeth and eating breakfast. A policy which might have made sense—probably *did,* probably *did*—hundreds of years ago. But (a sigh) it wasn't for him to take it upon himself to

hange things, although there was certainly no danger of
verpopulation *now*. No. Mustn't rock the boat. No point
n doing more than dropping a sort of hint, a mere specu-
ation, as it were, not even a suggestion. . . .

"In my report. Not the next one. The last one. Before
pension out. Have some grilled quirk?"

He pushed the tray-laden cart the hand's breadth
needed for Lomar to reach it without stirring. The name,
rather than the unfamiliar but pleasant taste of the crispy
seafood brought the afternoon's little adventure back to
Lomar's mind. *We'll have it with our supper,* she'd said.
He'd forgotten his appointment, she'd said no more about
hers. A strange girl . . . Fresh, new, good in bed, possibly dangerous. There must be others. Best to look
around before becoming too involved. Yes . . .

Much the best. . . .

The days passed, the long, long days of Pia 2. Now the
air was heavy and rank with curing redwing, now it was
fresh and had the tang of the sea, now it lay cool and
quiet and smelled of taranth-trees and *pi*-vines. Ran
Lomar never made his look-see trip, barely ever thought
about his plans of making it. Not that he was busy-busied
with his work, for he had no work. No other duties had
been assigned to him, and as for his formal, Guild-directed
duties, nothing ever seemed to come of them. And the
empty parade of Station life stood now revealed for the
silly little pomp it was: two hundred men pretending to
do the work which could have been done by two dozen
with time to spare.

He spent much time devising plans for the redwing and
much less time realizing why none of them would do,
working himself into torques and furies which put him
into prime shape for loving Lindel—

—if *love* was (it really wasn't, altogether, or very
much) if *love* was really the proper word for the bouts
and matches in which his frenzied, questing body was
pitted against hers and against time, when there seemed
no time, yet it seemed no time dared wait for time. And
then, afterwards, marvelously at peace, murmuring murmuring marvelous peace—

—when he could find her. Or when she chose to find
him.

One day when he couldn't or she didn't (forgotten his

prior notions of not getting too involved, his intention
of looking for other girls, women, maybe even Tocky
girls), enraged at his own inability to achieve the de-
tachment and disinterest that he felt could be so easily
attained when he came here; enraged at this as much
as at the Station which he found stupidly squared and
cubed, exceeding anything on Old Earth—what price now.
Escape?—in such a mood and on sudden impulse, he
took off on a shorter version of the long explorations he
had promised himself.

He put on field clothes, picked up a Tock guide, drew
rations for a few days easily enough, was charily issued
one (count it), one weapon by the reluctant armorer.
and found himself outside Station limits almost before
he grew calm again. It wasn't until the rasping noise of
the whip grass against his boots made him aware of the
reason why the Tocks always had rags bound around
their legs that he recognized the occasion for what it was
—a breach, a break.

A dividing mark.

Rango the guide, swinging his staff in one hand and his
hack in the other, said, as they approached the first
hill toward the South, "Ist good you gahst a gun."

Lomar grunted. Swung his staff and dug it into the
ground.

"Ist good fro *you*. I doe need em. I gahst a charm."
He nodded, tapped his chest proudly, where a leather
thong vanished under the ragged tunic.

"Yace. We seece a spider," spitting three times and
dabbing his toe, "you cah shoot em. You assen gah no
charm, you ber shoot em quick-quick. *Me*—I squahs
down, hole my charm, an I sace em words, you-know. Eh
spider cahn brahther me. No-no. I gesta charm, oh two-
three week ago. I gest em fro ladydoctor. Cost me losta
redwing, losta chist fro store." The spirit of enterprise,
seemingly, was far from extinct in Rango. For close to a
year he had made extra-special efforts, passing up big
drunks, paying to "the ladydoctor" most of the store chits
for the redwing he'd gathered.

A small flicker of interest arose in Lomar. If the desire
for a charm against rorks could do this for Rango, why
not for the other Tocks? The flicker died down. It
wouldn't work. Nothing would work.

From the hilltop, crowned with flowering purpleweed,

34

he took a final look at the Station. That small reticulation was all there was on this whole forsaken planet, of knowledge, science, civilization. And much it cared for any of it. Down a ways off was the jumbled scar of Tockeytown. What would happen—another thought like another spark flashed in his mind, made him jump a bit—what would happen if for any reason no more Q Ships ever came here?

For a moment he almost hoped it would happen. Let the whole stupid, frozen-minded clot of them perish. For damned sure, he wouldn't perish with them! Let them huddle and hope and wait and fall into decay, death, madness, despair, scanning the skies while things crumbled around them. But *he* wouldn't be there. Damn the Station, damn redwing, routine, closed minds and all of that. Plans, half-formed adventurous notions, wiggled and flapped in his mind. He would find the old maps, build a boat, find the other continents or islands. Lindel with him. . . . A few brighter Tocks. . . .

It wouldn't work. Nothing worked here.

Suppose, just suppose, he'd suggested, *that we pay the Tocks more for redwing. Then maybe they'd have an incentive to bring in more.*

Blank looks. The click of closing minds. *Wouldn't work couldn't work couldn't be done foolish damnfool notion no. Give the Tocks more know what they'd do they'd work less that's all. Give the Tocks a little food and fermentables they'll go on a bust as soon as the 'rot is ready they'll keep it up for days then they won't work for days afterward.*

Lomar and Rango planting their staves into the hillside, went on an angle down and along, down and along. Here and there on the yellow-green slopes crimson-scarlet splashes of redwing showed. Here and there a chipmunk-sized leaper hopped quickly from one clump of growth to the concealment of another. Station and Tockeytown alike fell out of sight and the staves served to balance the men as they made the stiff descent. Here and there a tumble of bark and branches—a housey—with sometimes a dirty face framed in matted hair. . . .

Give the Tocks more? *More* what? *Everything you give them has to come out of Station stores. Want* us *to do without so you can wrap their dirty hides in fine clothes?*

35

So much for giving the Tocks more, say, twice as much, in hopes they'd gather twice as much. What then? Give the Tocks only half as much——? in hopes they'd gather twice as much in order to make as much as they'd been making before?

No that's no good the stupid bastards would starve to death before they'd figure out what was what no no good nothing is any good lazy stupid

Here and there they passed gatherers—sometimes an individual, more often (as they got farther from the Station) a group—pulling up the redwing plants, making their bundles, dragging them back, singing their melancholy songs. But there were not many of them and, indeed, it seemed to Lomar that there was not exactly an abundance of redwing either. Was the whole fault entirely one of Tock laziness or incapacity? Had North Tockland been overgrazed, as it were? If so, why did the rank smell of the plant seem to stick in his nostrils?

They paused to eat and, later, to dip and splash and wash in a spring-fed pond half in the sunlight and half in the shadow; Rango giggling as if at some great joke as he succumbed to the unexpected experience of soap and lather. Washed and combed, but not yet clad in his rags again, Rango—for as long as a transient serious thought wiped the usual Tock grin from his face—might have been anybody, anyplace . . . not an "autochthonous person" but a "man."

Some remotely cognate thought was what had evidently just occurred to Rango, for, turning to Lomar, he said, "Youce a real man, yace."

"How's that?"

Rango's long arms waved with the effort of framing his thought in other words. "Youce fro Old Earth."

"Oh, yes. I am."

Rango nodded with satisfaction. "Yace. Youce a *real* man. Comes fro Old Earth. . . ."

Ran was mildly tickled at this conceit or fancy of the unlettered Tock, but not sufficiently so as to want to trace it to its source. He got to his feet, Rango scrambled up, they dressed and went on. The last part of last afternoon was spent in a sidewise ascent of an interminable upthrust of the land, barbed with raw rock. Once, as they paused to relieve themselves, Rango said, "Mist Ran—this Last Ridge."

Ran grunted something about being damn glad it *was* the last, and the knowledge put a little fresh vigor into his tired leg muscles. He hadn't even lifted his eyes for a long time when Rango stopped and drew in his breath with a hiss. Slowly, Lomar raised his head. His glance followed the guide's pointing finger.

From where they then stood the terrain sloped gently enough into a shallow bowl, and beyond the rim of the bowl it vanished. Past there and an incalculable distance beyond and below stretched a great plain towards the misty horizon where the land fused with the sky.

And to the right and to the left, before and behind, as far as the marveling eye could reach, all the land was blazing and aflame with redwing.

For many minutes the sheer wonder of it—the great empty heart of the neglected and all but unknown continent—and the sheer beauty of it—held him silent. And then (afterwards he was to reproach himself for it, curse the fact . . . if it was a fact . . . that he was a Guildsman at heart; seek excuses like "medical necessity"; recall the instructor at the Academy: "What is Man, young aspirants? Man is an animal that trades . . .") and then, almost explosively, angrily—

"Why don't you gather your redwing *there*?

"There! There!

"Look at it! It must be as thick as grass! Why—"

And Rango looked at him with openmouthed, gap-toothed astonishment. "Why . . . Why, Mist Ran . . . Why, this all *rork* country! This Rorkland! Whence Cold Time, *then* wece goin. But nah now, Mist Ran. Nah now."

Rorkland! All rork country. And the rork was the bogeyman, the curse, the devil, and the terror-in-the-night.

"Are there any down there now, do you think? Any rorks? In sight?"

"Ah. Spiders. You wahn see em. Yace. Inna lookin-glahs."

Looking glass . . . surely Rango didn't mean a mirror? Was he supposed to turn around and gaze in a reflection? Did the rork turn the viewer to stone, like Medusa? Not till the Tock pointed to the farseer, did Lomar understand. He unbuckled the case at his belt and lifted the instrument to his eyes. Haze leapt into clarity. The redwing was no longer a single massy carpet, but, still, the plants appeared more thickly, were visibly larger, than they were in Tockland.

And then, by that curious little trick of the mind, whereby we often (or so it seems) become aware of the sound of an engine just the merest moment before it stops, so Ran Lomar observed the rork only in the second before it rose and walked. His first rork!

How large was it, he could not say, having nothing to measure it against but the redwing, and in that excited moment no longer sure at all that the plants at that distance were really larger. Like a great black boulder, it seemed, shading into dark grey below. Spider! Yes, that would have been the obvious comparison, and the term would lead to no confusion since Pia 2 was without arachnids of its own. There was no separate head, and the body was underslung, lower than the knees of the creature's legs, so that it hung—so to speak—from its own thighs, rather than being supported upon them. A daddy longlegs type of animal, with body much larger in proportion to legs than that harmless wee creature of Old Earth (still quietly surviving when all the great saurians and mammals had passed off the scene, the elephant as extinct as the baluchitherium), and . . . legs . . . yes. There was no doubt of it. In this respect, at least, the old books were right. The roark was quadruped.

This one now proceeded to shake itself, then to groom itself first with one long, limber foot and then, by turn, the others. Then it paused as if listening. Now he could see the stalked eyes. Then it moved leisurely down the ranks of redwing until it was partially concealed and he could not see what it was doing when it stopped. The body dipped a bit. A frond of redwing shivered, shook, seemed to shoot up, then down. The rork came fully into sight again, the plant in its mouth . . . he assumed that was its mouth. . . . If the beast would only turn—

It turned, giving him for the first time a clear sight of the so-called "mask." Difficult to believe that this was not a face! The yellow markings, enclosed in a sort of cartouche of the same color, so perfectly counterfeiting eyes, nose, mouth: but, whatever it was, it was no face. The eyes, like a snail's, were on top. The old books said that the rork breathing outlet was on top, too. And the mouth lay well beneath the bottom line of the mask.

As he watched, something appeared at the mouth,

dropped to the ground. He thought it was a root, could not be sure. The great red leaf trembled and, as the rork munched and mumbled the stalk, was drawn slowly towards the indistinct dark cavern of the mouth—

Rango jostled his arm. The rork was lost to sight. Angered, Lomar turned to the guide, who, not looking at him, pointed below, much closer by.

"Sst, Mist Ran—aim the lookin glass down there . . . you seece eh big-big tree near brook?"

Lomar, after a moment, did. In the farseer, so quickly that he gave a start, appeared an animal utterly unlike a rork, and much, much smaller. Something was in its mouth, either a small leaper or a large crybaby, perhaps. It was there but an instant, then, suddenly, it scuttled away. First another, then another, the same kind of creature, passed rapidly before his gaze. The grass quivered a bit. Then nothing more. After another minute he put down the farseer.

"What you seece, Mr. Ran?" the Tock demanded—somewhat anxiously, it seemed. "Rips?"

"Was that what they were? Long and low?"

His guide nodded vigorously, his long, dark, now clean hair shaking. "Yace. Rips . . . How many you seece?"

"Three of them . . . why?"

"Three? No more? For-sure?"

Lomar assured him there were no more. The Tock reflected, clearly—by his expression—uncertain whether this was good or bad. Then he gestured towards Pia Sol, whose sullen blood-orange disk seemed to hover just a bit over the horizon. "Time to goce make a housey for hide en sleep."

Rango took considerable pains, stripping the loose, soft bark from chosen trees, trimming branches with his hack; but it was small enough for all that, and had to be entered on hands and knees. Lomar was glad that they had both bathed. Rango insisted on making a fire despite the heater and the ward lamp in Lomar's field pack, and, as they sat by it after supper, he began to talk.

One star was brighter than all in that black sky, blazing with a blue-white brilliance while the crybabies wailed and sobbed all around them. Rango flung out his hand towards it. "Old Earth," he said, awe in his voice.

"What's that?" Lomar was startled.

"Old Earth, Old Earth."

"World as gives our fathers birth,
"Wish a-may, wish a-might,
"Haves the wish a-wish tonight,"

chanted Rango.

It was, of course, Lomar very well knew, nothing of the sort. It was Pia 3, the ball of slag officially known as Ptolemy Philadelphius, but unofficially called (in the cleaned-up version) "The Dung Heap." But, being touched by both the fellow's innocence and the verse which, in one form or another, was old when "our fathers" were still bound to the surface of their native world, he would not for the world have disillusioned him. The Tocks had little enough; they had, in fact, almost nothing.

Except this.

Had it been possible to plunge at once that next morning into the rufous jungle below, Lomar might have done it. But the descent of the off side of Last Ridge was obviously even a heavier undertaking than the ascent of the nigh side had been. Rango's frequent noisy swallowing and thong-clutching as they viewed the prospect showed that he was probably far from anxious to put his new-bought charm to the test. And then, suddenly, suddenly, it seemed to Lomar that he had to find out a lot more about the rorks before meeting any of them face (so to speak) to face.

Up till now it had seemed that the Tocks were the one and the only key to the redwing matter. Now it seemed that there was another key—the rorks.

Rango received the sudden change of plans with relief, and hastened eagerly into talk. "Yace, Mist Ran, no-good now. You waist an see—comes Cold Time, wece goin nen. Nen spiders changen skins. Assen gahst no strengths. Lossa Tocks, some men, too, wece comin down to Rorkland. You come, too, Mist Ran. You come, too."

And Lomar had thought that it might not be until then that he would be coming back to Last Ridge and its tremendous views.

But he was wrong.

The Station Library echoed to his steps. It was free enough of dust and dirt, the clean up Tocks saw to that. But no one was there. Catalogs, stacks and files were open to his touch. The two viewing rooms were as empty

40

as the rest of the place. He threaded the spools to allow for continuous showing, sat back in his seat and depressed the cam on the arm of the chair.

Some of the spools were text clear through, others were 3D and narrative. The words had been written, and the voices spoken, by men and women long, long dead, and were marked throughout with little touches of the archaic. Nothing had been done to add to the material for centuries. However, there was no reason to assume that the rorks were any different now than they were then. And the unworn condition of the repro now unfolding before his eyes gave no reason to assume that many people had ever been interested in learning about them.

There it was, in three dimensions, sound, and color: Rorkland. And there were the rorks, much better, clearer, longer views than he'd gotten with just his farseer. ". . . *fearfully intelligent*. . . ." Now, that was odd . . . He watched with bemused fascination a speed-up of the skin-shedding process the creatures gradually went through in winter, as they lay in their nests, moving sluggishly, when at all. Why, if the ancient observers had been correct,—why, if the rork were strictly herbivorous and attacked only in self-defense, should they be described as *fearfully* intelligent? Had the author-narrator been suspicious that his contemporaries were wrong and others right?—that the rork ate men, as well as attacking them on sight? And did they indeed venture into Tockland to capture human babies for a more grisly diet than mere redwing?

There was something stirring, tragic, in the views of the original settlers, forebears of the Tocks: clean, alert, vigorous, full of intelligence and zeal. To what had their descendents come!

He emerged from the library slowly and thoughtfully. And to find the Station in an uproar.

No one, that month, thought of redwing at all. The Tocks came pouring in from all quarters of their small homeland—some of them from so far off that their grubby-faced and naked brats screamed in terror at the strange sight of Station personnel. The force fields were set up and all Guildsmen supplied with arms and—wonder of wonders!—Manton, the Motor Aide, even parted with several of his precious skimmers. And Edran Lomar found himself in one of them with Tan Carlo Harb, the Station Officer.

The shrill sound of the alarm still seemed to echo in his ears as he looked over the side. Height had been set for ten feet as soon as the vehicle passed out of the treelined streets. "I'm a rather good shot at rips," the SO said, "but when things are like this, there's no point in trying for individual kills. No sport in it when you can hardly miss. . . . I'm upping speed, boy. Hold on. Hold . . . on."

After the lurch the ride was smooth again. "How often are things like this?" Lomar asked. "When the rips swarm?"

A new light was in the SO's eyes, a new color in his cheeks. "Oh, every so often," he said, vaguely. "If the north end of the continent wasn't on a plateau, things would be much worse. As it is, well, to tell you the truth, it's chiefly a rather exciting but hardly a dangerous period. Not for us. Gives us a chance to get the kinks out of our buttocks and the stale air out of our lungs, run around and skim around and shout . . . and all that. *Ha!* Look there! Below, left—*there!*"

There, where the SO's plump finger pointed, a bush seemed suddenly to explode as at least a dozen leapers sprang out of it. And springing after them were the yellow-grey brindled bodies of the rips. They were perhaps no larger than large hares, and in shape were not very much unlike them, save for the batlike ears and stiff, erect tails. One of the leapers alone managed to make its escape, its great, terrified bounds covering at least five meters at a time. While other rips ravaged and worried their prey, another set off in pursuit, teeth bared, clods of earth flying from the sharp and non-retractable claws capable of the dreadful damage which gave the beast its name.

"Hold control," the SO said, abruptly, pressing the release toggle. Lomar hastily activated the instrument set on his side. Scarcely had he time to notice Harb seizing the weapon, when it snapped, releasing the tiny but telltale little burst of mist, and the rip—already dead—stumbled, whirled, and fell.

"Not bad," said the SO. "Return control."

Lomar looked back to see the rip pack tearing the

42

ody of its mate to bloody pieces. One of them raised
. reddened snout and seemed to gaze back toward him
with milky eyes. He shuddered.

"Lemmings," said Harb, his voice reflecting satisfac-
ion.

"Sir?"

"Don't you know the natural history of your own
world, Lomar? *Lemmings.* An extinct mammal that
lved in Iceland or Greenland . . . was it Scotland? . . .
ever mind, doesn't matter. Lemmings; I've been trying
o think of that name ever since I stepped into the
kimmer. I thought that you'd be able to tell me some-
hing about them. Too bad. Well. The lemmings used
o swarm now and then, just as the rips do. Something
bout their metabolism, or am I thinking of something
lse? Suddenly they'd increase in numbers, incredible,
remendous increase. And then they'd pour out, over-
unning the country until, according to the quaint old
egends, they would reach the sea—"

"I bet that stopped them."

"If so, Lomar, you would lose your money. No, as a
natter of fact—or fancy, as it may be—that did *not*
top them. They had swum across ponds and lakes and
ivers and so they assumed—one would suppose—that
he ocean was just another of the same. So, in they'd
lunge, millions and millions of them," Harb said, en-
husiastically, "and swim until they drowned. . . . Oh,
 suppose some of them must have gotten back to shore
r else never went in the water at all, otherwise there
vould've been no more to carry on the species. But the
ips, on the other hand—see them? Look. See? See? In-
red-ible."

Pack after pack passed beneath them as they skimmed
outhward. They ate the crybabies taking their diurnal
leep, they devoured the leapers as they fled, they con-
umed the slow and the harmless and they lapped up
he ordinary carnivores of the North country with little
nore difficulty. The rips crunched nestlings and fledgings
nd jumped, again and again, after birds and daybats on
he wing. Several times several of them lunged and tore at
he shadow of the skimmer on the ground, and sprang
oward the craft itself.

A grunt of alarm escaped Lomar as the rips hurtled
loft, bared muzzles exposing bloody tushes, glazed and

seemingly sightless eyes staring insanely. Harb gave a quick burble of amusement. "We're ten feet up," he said, "although it may not seem so. They can't jump more than half that distance. Oho—Last Ridge up ahead. We'l skim down and take a look at Upper Rorkland a bit You'll see something there!

"And don't let the fact that your testicles have probably retreated bother you . . . If I didn't know tha' Starchy Manton watches over every gear, sprocket, diode and transducer in these vessels as if they were parts o: his own tender flesh I wouldn't risk my ass flying two feet over the nursery; certainly not over all the swarming rips in Creation; *hold* on!"

The skimmer slid down the angle of the air. Ran Lomar held on tightly, opened his eyes wide. Scarlet-crimson and huge were the redwing leaves in the great valley of the rorks, but what held his attention—gripped it, would no' let it go—was the great wave that advanced slanting up the valley. A greyish-yellow wave—

"There they are," said Harb, in a low voice. "Can you count them? You can count the stars, maybe, but no' them."

The rips seemed to have no end to their numbers None at all. On and on came the wave, the skimme: hovering where she stood, the wave boiling and moiling beneath, onward and onward—

"Oh," said Harb. "Look you there. I've heard it. I didn't believe it. I'm not sure I believe it now."

"What? What?"

"The Tocks have always said it. But I never saw it I never saw it before. Oh, look—"

Where he pointed and where Lomar looked was a line a thin line, of great dark forms, bounding and leaping on spidery legs; charging forward ahead of the grea' grey-yellow wave of rips.

"The Tocks told me. They often told me. 'The rork, they said . . . 'The rork lead them on. They lead them on to attack us'."

And the wave rolled on, rolled on, and broke upor the gaunt and granite-hard escarpment of the cliffs o: Last Ridge.

The difficult ascent of the Ridge limited the number of the swarming predators that could make their way onto the plateau. Limited—but did not stop them. Stories were told of entire Tock families devoured alive, of screaming fugitives trapped and overwhelmed within very near reach of the force fields which so safely ringed around the Station, the great generators smoothly toiling to their tasks. And one or two or a few more, attacked by single beasts, were able to defend themselves with their hacks, slashing the slashers.

For almost a month the seemingly endless swarms of rips rolled on out of the unknown interior. They reached the sea, but did not plunge into it to their destruction. There they mated, as was their practice in every breeding season, and there they laid their eggs, leathery clusters of them, and covered them with sand.

And then, afterward, for hundreds of miles, up and down the ragged shores of the sullen sea, in great numbers they died.

The silence seemed long and unnatural.

The Tocks trooped back to the outlands with much less despatch than they had fled therefrom. For those of them who had reached safety in time the whole period had been much of a lark; fed from Guild stores (reluctantly, but fed nonetheless), they had been free from their labors to roam the streets of the small settlement which was to them Babylon the Great—not that they had ever heard of it—but now it was all over.

"Some of them had the brass to turn up at the Store today for rations," Second Aide Arlan told Lomar, with an outraged titter. "Sent them away with a flea in their ear—'Gather redwing, confound you,' the fellow told them. 'Holiday is over. Chop weed if you want to eat'."

And gather redwing they did. For a while. But then there was an outbreak of Tock fever.

And production dropped to almost nothing.

CHAPTER THREE

The Cape of Smokes, it was said, marked the beginning of South Tockland. The name, Ran had vaguely thought, referred to some volcanic activity, past or present. But it became clear enough as the Station's single, small watercraft came abaft of the Cape that the tiny wisp of white which presently appeared was man-made.

"Signal," said the quartermaster. "They'll be waiting for us."

"Welcoming committee?" asked Ran. But the QM only grunted.

The utter failure of Lomar's efforts with the Tame Tocks had thrown him into a depression which passed, in turn, to indifference. He went on a camp-out trip with Lindel, but it had not lasted long. It was pleasant for a while around their fire in the crisp autumnal air, but when she had tried to rally him to return to his work, he had lost his temper. What work? he demanded, angrily? Let him alone . . . And she had. So completely, in fact, that when he returned from a long and sullen walk she was gone.

Then he and Reldon had gone on a joint drunk together which left him with a bad hangover and a hot, confused memory of musky revels with a pubescent but artful Tocky girl.

All in all, it seemed time for some sort of change.

The redwing output of South Tockland had never amounted to as much as the highest production of the North; but, then, neither had it ever fallen below the lowest. He'd failed on what was, so to speak, home ground. What had he to lose by looking over things at the continent's other end?

"Nothing that I can think of," admitted SO Harb, plucking meditatively at his plump lower lip. "Don't imagine that it will do much, if any, good either. All that they want down there are guns and gunmakings. They'd like us to issue them standard Guild weapons, if you please, you know. Ostensibly to kill rorks so the gathering can be safer—actually, to pursue their rotten little feuds of wars. Fat chance, ha. There's only one place, after all, this whole savage world over, where they could get ammunition fit for standard weapons, and that's right here. So every weapon the Station supplied them would forever be aimed, in the long run, right at our own heads.

"*Ergo*, thank you, but *no*, thank you. However . . . speaking of guns reminds me. There is one chap, cute, down in South Barbaria or South Savageland, who might be of some help to you, personally. Name of . . . name
46

of . . . Fout, I can't remember it. Squawman. Used to be Station armorer. Look him up. And now, another wee drinkie? . . ."

Hardly could the inhabitants be wilder than their own untamed coastland, Ran Lomar thought, as they rounded Cape of Smokes. He examined the black, bleak fiords through his farseer, hoping to line up on something human or of human provenance. The smoke, however, issued up from among a mass of broken rocks from which the fire's makers could see without being seen. Not until they were well South did he see anything of the sort he was looking for—a long, thin boat of the open type, its bow riding high out of the water and a man at the stern with a steering oar. There was a stumpy mast and a ragged sail held by a cord on which a ragged boy had his hand.

So much he could see from afar, but they came close by after a while. The Tame Tocks had no seacraft of any kind. But a glance sufficed to tell, had Ran been in doubt, that these were no Tame Tocks. The boy had the bushy-browed look of a man, and the man had the seamed and sunken features of an old man, though his black hair and straight back showed he was not. Their odd clothes were old, but totally without the unmistakable and slummy look of Tame Tocks' clouts.

When the two vessels were near enough for him to see all this with his naked eye, Ran waved and called in greeting. The eyes of the man and boy in the boat moved toward him as he did so. But it was their eyes alone which moved.

"Friendly," said the quartermaster.

"The South Tockland navy, I suppose," Lomar said, nettled.

That one long, lonesome craft had been bound on some private mission of its own—perhaps one of simple transportation, easy enough to understand if the interior was anything like the coast. But as the Station's small ship stood on down the coast it passed a number of other boats, and all these were fishing craft. They were not, however, in the least more friendly. And, from cape to cape, headland to headland, and, finally, angling over land in a way which Lomar realized would be heading straight toward the tiny port town without the necessity

47

of rounding the coast, the warning smokes of the signal fires went up ahead of them.

The wind got through him, by and by—it was the Cold Time and he went below to brood and drink and give his scant gear one last going-over.

The harbor was a good enough one for rafts, catamarans, and dugouts—a few specimens of all were seen —but it was not one in which the quartermaster cared to risk his ship.

"A boat may come out for you," he said, with an air of finality.

"And if it doesn't?"

The QM shrugged. "Can you swim?" he asked.

Finally a boat did come out, with, at the stern paddle, what might have been a twin brother of the steersman in the first Wild craft they'd passed—lank black hair, lantern jaw, seamed and sunken cheeks, and grim immobile face. It was not on him, however, that Lomar's eyes rested, but on the only other man aboard. It could only have been "the squawman" of whom Tan Carlo Harb had spoken. He was white-haired, erect, and though his expression was serious, it was quite devoid of the constitutional dourness of the Wild Tock behind him. He wore what had once been Guildsman's uniform, without any insigne, and scoured almost white with many washings.

"Guildsman, what hail?" he called—and climbed aboard without waiting to be answered.

"Hello, Old Guns," the QM said; then inclined his head toward Lomar. "Fellow wants to come ashore, stay awhile."

The older man surveyed him calmly, then put out his hand. "Jacs Calzas," he said. "Former rating of—but never mind that. 'Old Guns' will do. It's done for this long."

The Station ship—it had no name and needed none, there being no others to confuse it with—besides its semiannual circumnavigation of the continent, carried the old pensioner the purchases he was allowed to make from the Guild store up North. It also brought him, and this, its first trip since the Q had come and quickly gone, what little mail there was for him. All was quickly enough placed in the boat along with Lomar's gear.

48

"Come ashore," Old Guns urged the quartermaster, "and have a gam. I haven't got a bad place here. . . ."

But the QM shook his head. Old Guns and Lomar went ashore alone. They were halfway across the harbor when Ran thought of saying goodbye, but when he turned around the ship was already gone.

"They don't care to tarry, somehow," Old Guns said. "Though I can't think why. . . ." Some dry note in his voice indicated that he wasn't to be taken altogether seriously.

Black was the predominate color, as it seemed to be throughout all of, at least coastal, South Tockland. Black were the hills out of which the harbor bowl had been scoured, black were the trees clutching grimly to the grim black rocks, black were the few huddled houses ahead of them, and black the very waters over which they rode.

". . . but it damned well suits me. I live back in the hills at my clan-seat . . . actually, my old wife's clan-seat . . . no, damn it! mine, too. It's a thin, hard, cold life, but there's something clean and pure about it— like a drink of well water first thing in the early morning. If it weren't for the fevers and the feuds— But there's plenty of time to talk, plenty of time."

The skimpy pier of thin black poles drew closer, closer. The thin black boat skimmed along the dimpling surface. There were a number of people, mostly men and children, on the shore. The air was cold and damp and smelled of wetness, woodsmoke, and fish.

"I spent the better, which is to say, the worst part of twenty years up north at that nest of flatulent fools, and I hated every minute of it. One day a troop of Wild men came sailing up to trade. There was nothing of the Noble Savage about them, but I knew—the second I saw them—that they were for real. I'd have given my pension for the chance to go back with them, right then. And I came down the first chance I could, and I kept on coming down, every chance I could. And when I pensioned out I settled here to stay. And here's where I'll be buried."

It seemed sure that they'd hit the pier, but the paddle splashed in the water, someone caught the flung rope just when it appeared certain that nobody would, and they came to rest at the foot of a rude ladder. In a low, musing voice, Old Guns said, "It hasn't been easy. . . ."

The Mister Mallardy had been dying slowly for years and saw only a few members of his own household. But his heir-son had had a long time to take hold, and things in Mallardy Camp were held firm and went well enough. The walls and fences were in sound repair, the roofs and boats scarcely leaked any more than was only natural, and from every tar-black homestead arose at least a single thread of smoke; and from some, several —a sure sign of at least modest prosperity when all the firestones were fed.

What the interiors of the other households might be like, Ran had as yet no idea; but the Old Guns' house was certainly far from typical, with its mixture of the civilized and the barbaric: a Guild-issue bed lined neatly against a wall on which a rork-skin was pegged, a small case of books and on top of it two pikeheads and a whetstone, a worktable with a tiny solar motor and a number of modern tools, a dismantled something-or-other which seemed to be an archaic firearm of a sort, a roughhewn trestle table on which was set a tray of glasses. . . . So it went.

"My position here would be stronger, in one way, if I had a son instead of a daughter," Old Guns observed, setting down his pack with a short sigh. "But if I had, he'd surely be involved in some feud or other, so I'm just as glad. Also, my wife is close kin to The Mister, and my son—if I had one—would be an heir of sorts and there'd be jealousy. So I'm content with just Norna. The child of my old age. Not that I ever had a child in my earlier age. Things are somewhat in a slump around here now, with the fever abroad. I wanted to take Norna up North when she was a tot and have her given general immunity. But I was told that it couldn't be done . . . they count her as a Tock, too, of course, damn it. Oh, well. She feeds better than most around here—I see to it—and keeps herself and the house cleaner than most, and so far she's stayed fairly well in health.

"Let's pull up chairs and get warm . . ."

Old Guns had fitted up a sort of stove of scrap-metal, and the room was not only warmer than it would have been if only heated by a firestone, it was free of smoke, too.

"Now," said Old Guns, having thrust several sticks of wood, furry with black moss, into the stove; "what's *your* problem?"

He listened to Lomar's story in silence broken only by mmms and hmms. Then he got up and stretched. "Shall we dine?" he asked. And then waited not for an answer, but called out, *"Eats!"*

Almost immediately the doorway curtain was thrust aside and two women entered with trays and cloths. He introduced them, as they were setting the table. "My old wife, Sathy. My daughter, Norna. Take a seat, Ranny." The two women looked very much alike, with their very white skins, straight backs, snapping black eyes and black hair fastened behind. "Old," as a description of Sathy, was more affection than accuracy. A few gray hairs, a few fine lines near eyes and mouth, no more.

"Yes, she holds up well," Old Guns commented, noting his guest's glance and reading his thoughts. "I picked a good one to start off with, for one thing, and I've used her as a wife and a friend, not a damned slave and beast of burden. The others, you know, the Wild Tocks, they trot their wives till they're withered and feeble. Then they prop them up in the chimney corners and make household gods and oracles out of them. They have an easy old age—'easy,' as things go down here—if they live that long.

"But this one's got quite a lot of jump and spark left in her, yet. Haven't you, old besom?"

"Put your eats in your mouth," the old besom said, unruffled.

"Not yet, you heathen." He said a brief grace. Then he served the food. Over the chowder, broiled fish, and tataplants they talked of many things. In theory, and if one were writing a romance, the presence of Old Guns, with his superior knowledge and technical training, might have sparked some sort of renascence among the Wild Tocks. In plain and unfanciful fact, however, nothing of the sort had taken place. Old Guns had no missionary notions any more than anyone else in his time had. Even if he possessed them, the people he now lived among would not have been receptive, being just as narrow and rigid in their own way as anyone else. The

51

small solar motor which he'd bought with his own money was able, during the rarer-than-not sunny days which South Tockland afforded, to charge itself for the few small tasks he used it for. His duties, when station armorer, had been exclusively concerned with simple maintainance. The abrupt change in attitude indicated by his deciding to live among "the Wild people" was the only change he'd ever made; indeed, was likely the only one of which he'd been capable.

A faint tradition of artisanship and social structure did indeed survive here in the South, though the country's limited resources and periodic feuding and petty wars arrested much of even such mutual aid as the people were capable of. The clan system depended not only on ties of blood but on the number of matchlocks each clan's "Mister" was able to muster, and the matchlocks were made and repaired from the few scraps of metal gotten in trade for redwing; how much redwing they gathered depended on how many people they had in the first place, and how many of these could be spared from other work—gardening, fishing, and so on—and from feuding. Charcoal they made for themselves with difficulty; nitrate or saltpetre they were able to supply in one nasty way or another involving the husbandry of their own body wastes, but sulphur—the third essential ingredient for the crude black power that fired their 'lock guns—they had to obtain from the Guild Station.

And the Guild Station did not have an unlimited supply, and its price came high.

"But you mustn't think," the squawman said, earnestly, "that they look upon their 'locks just as instruments for pushing up one clan and pushing down another. When they go out to gather redweed they go out in force, full truce, and every match is lit and every eye is open for rorks. Little weed grows in these hills and so it has to be gone for into Rorkland, you see. And the toll comes high. Yes . . . the toll comes high. My old wife lost two cousins last year. If there'd been more 'locks on hand to protect them, they might not have been killed. It's a constant source of bitterness, because they know full well that they could all be supplied with arms if the Guild allowed. They are bitter, and they are proud."

So proud that they refused to trade for the Station's

52

cast-off clothes, which was all the Tame Tocks wore; and made their own of skins and beaten bark.

"A few of them keep the knowledge of reading, you know—"

"No," said Ran, surprised. "I didn't." No Tame Tock could read.

"Yes. . . . They can hardly afford the cost, but they do buy up bits of scrap paper when they come to trade, and they commemorate their own history, such as it is and has been. I find that touching, you know." By reading those rude "books," Old Guns had learned much—including details of that dreadful period, the memory of which had burned and scarred, when for long, long years not a single ship had put down on Pia 2 and the forebears of the Tocks had been alone, quite alone . . .

And had starved and fought and died.

"I found something curious," Ran said, after a silence during which the two women had exchanged a smouldering glance or two. "Do you know, I think the Tame Tocks tend to, well, sort of *honor* me? Because I come from the old homeworld, from Old Earth."

Promptly, "Well, you won't find it so, here," Old Guns said. "On the contrary—so keep your mouth shut about it—they'd hate you for it. They blame Old Earth for the 'long lonesome' which ruined things to begin with. Old Earth sent them, Old Earth didn't protect them, Old Earth ignores them. . . . Some even say that the fever came from there. I don't know, myself. Never been there. I'm a Coulter boy, though I'll never see that system again and I don't care."

He looked around his black-walled house, at his disparate possessions, at his wife and daughter, at the rugged landscape misting in the light rain through the open and unglazed window.

"No . . ." And he said again, "I don't care."

He had, so to speak, broken bread with them; and afterwards Sathy began to speak to him, asking him about his family: if his mother and father were alive, if he had brothers and sisters, and such like questions. When, later on that afternoon, the camp began to stir and a number of visitors arrived, Sathy took herself off to her tasks. But Norna remained, and sat next to him on a bench off to one side of the room and spoke to him in

53

a low voice and pointed out some chief personages.

"The Mister Dominis . . . directs six 'locks and twenty pike . . . yeh, the big whitebeard; brings good men to the fight, good men in his country. . . ." *Country* being the district, thinly inhabited, of which he was chief; so much had the old terms shrunk. No one had been attending to the fire and in the growing chill Lomar became conscious of the warmth of the girl next to him, and various thoughts and images began to enter his mind. He dismissed them. He wasn't yet aware of what the local attitude towards that sort of thing might be, and had no desire to find himself pegged out beneath a redwing plant to see for himself what sort of diet the rorks *really* had.

Her long hair brushed his ears as she turned to him again. "And at his next, the Mister Hannit, directing ten 'lock and twenty-seven pike. But he pledged two, or was it it three, 'locks to the Mister Dominis a pair-o'-year back, and there's be trouble there yet, you know, Ranny."

A voice was raised in anger. "That's our Mister's heir-son, Jun Mallardy," she whispered. "He's wanted me for his woman, but I doesn't fancy him, you know."

Jun was rope-thin, black-bearded. "I knows it," he said loudly, now. "We's all knows it. Who's it as'd rather raid than farm 'r fish? Flinders! Who's it goes about with's dirty mouth to every ear, spitting talk and spitting trouble? Flinders! Muck-Hell, yes! Flinders breaks truce, Flinders is a rork's egg—and when I s'll be Mister here, I s'll tell him, same. But he doesn't lack gut, no. Says, he be's wrong in this? No!"

Some heads nodded, others were shaken dubiously; other voices were lifted, spoke together and drowned each other out. A sullen silence fell, abruptly. Old Guns, in a calming tone, said a few words. Jun grunted, did not appear convinced, but held his peace. "I have a guest— you see him sitting next to Norna on the bench," said Old Guns. "His name is Ran Lomar, and the Guild Misters have sent him here from Outside to see if he can get more redweed made."

All eyes turned toward Lomar, who arose and said, "It would help all of us . . ."

The great white beard of the Mister Dominis was thrust forward. "Never has the Guild Misters helped us. They's leaved our dad's dads here to eat the dirt and feed the rorks," he rumbled. "More redweed, says? Ha! They makes medicines with weed, but does they give it here? No! And so we perishes with fever. . . ."

A mutter of assent went around the group.

"Be's they going to give us guns or gunmakings for more weed?" demanded someone so young as to be still beardless, but whose close likeness to the thick-browed and hooknosed face of the Mister Hannit left little doubt that he was his son; and again there was the mutter of assent.

With intended tact, Lomar began to talk of ways that production could be increased; if the gatherers would hack off the redwing stalks as soon as they pulled the plant, then their loads would be lighter—

The men laughed scornfully. "We knows that the Tame turds as licks your dirty plates up to North hasn't the sense to do that," young Hannitt said. "But we has. And we does. What's else ye has to tell us, Guildsman?"

Nonplussed, he had nothing else at that moment to tell them, and while he stood there, gaping, the Wild men turned away from him. Angered at his own incapacity and at their insolent indifference, so different from the deference which the Tame Tocks accorded, he felt his rage coloring his face. While they muttered and grunted together, he thrust aside the curtain and passed through the anteroom to the outdoors.

The camp—every Wild Tock town was called a "camp"—stood on a hilltop from which, through a break in the black cascade of cliffs to the South, the ocean could be seen, the black dot of a boat passing slowly along.

The wind was wet and cold and grew colder. Three women passed along the trail below, bent beneath their loads of firewood; a boy came out of a low-roofed hut with several small and gutted fish impaled on a stick and took them into another. Most of the houses huddled together, some almost touching. Spindly, shrill children ran along the narrow lanes; and a half-grown boy, seeing Lomar looking on, numbly, spat in his direction, and wiped his mouth on his ragged sleeve. The "Wild" Tocks! Was there anything more for him here in the rugged South than in the dull North? There did not seem to be. There did not seem to be at all.

Presently the visitors and their host emerged together from Old Guns' house, and went down the winding path to the palisaded enclosure around the largest building in the camp—the Mister Mallardy's. In another moment the thin feather of smoke from the main smoke hole thickened. And, as if waiting only for this signal, a white flake drifted down from the leaden skies; then another, then the air was filled with them.

Whether to see the unfamiliar sight, or whether to punish himself for his own ineptitude, or to defy the fates which were bent on defying him and all his aims, he did not know; but Lomar stayed on and stayed on and on. He had some dim notion of waiting until dark, but the recollection that day on Pia 2 was six hours longer than on Old Earth, his distant, terribly distant home-world, worked its way up to the surface of his unhappy mind. And so, finally, cold and stiff and wet and almost past misery, he painfully made his way back the way he had come.

It was late when his host returned. He added his own damp clothing to his guest's, drying before the stove, and changed. Then, not looking over to where Lomar sat brooding in a corner chair, he said, "You think that redwing is the main problem?"

"What?"

"You think that getting more redwing is the main problem—don't you?"

Lomar frowned, blinked, yawned. Stretching, he asked, "It is for me, I guess. Why?"—suddenly becoming aware of the challenging and troubled tone of Old Guns' voice—"Isn't it?"

The elder man shook his head. Seating himself before the fire, he said, as if thinking aloud, "Suppose they could be convinced? I say, *suppose*. . . . What could they do? Mount an expedition and come on down here? No. No good. No good at all. No good if it could succeed, no good if it failed. Choice of evils. What then? Stay up there and wait? Keep the force fields up? For how—"

"Guns, what are you talking about?"

A stick of wood caught fire with little gouts and gusts of flame, blue bursts at first, then an audible burning, red and orange and yellow. Old Guns' craggy face was lit by the flickering light.

"For how long? Sooner or later they'd have to rest the generators. No. . . . No. . . . Whichever way I look at it: No." He stood up, abruptly. "Well— 'Come day, go day, God send Sunday,' and every day we've all got to eat. *Sathy? Norna?*"

And he wouldn't repeat what he'd been saying, or enlarge upon or explain any of it.

"Rorks," he said, after supper, taking up a pikehead and a whetstone. "They don't know anything about rorks up North. Down here we do. Know them as well as we know the lot at Flinders Crag. But— They can talk, boy. Listen, now. They can *talk!* I don't mean the Flinders, I mean the rorks. Oh, laugh, if you like. I didn't believe it either, when I first heard it. But it's true."

In a low voice, Ran said, "You've been down here too long."

Anger flashed in Norna's eyes at that. "And I says ye hasn't been here long enough! They can talk! They's been heard to! And what's more, they has a city—"

"Oh, come on!" he burst out, half-annoyed, half-amused. "I know better than that! I've seen them myself, and I've seen old 3Ds of them, too. A city, indeed!"

Norna's father nodded, slowly. "To be sure, it's hard to credit. They *have* been heard to talk. No one's seen their city in the daytime, but its lights have been seen at night from a place called Tiggy's Hill, far into Rorkland. Folks don't usually venture there, but now and then they do, in gathering; and they camp out on the Hill and build guard fires all around and keep a watch and ward, you may be sure, main carefully. And at such times they have seen the windows and streets of a great city. . . . This place is called the Plain of Lights. And if it isn't rorks that live there—and I'm not sure, for one— then, tell me who does? People? So great a place would require a great area of fields to feed, and would have a great population. We've seen no signs of such. No—don't underestimate the rork, Ranny. Don't underestimate them at all."

That night, sleeping on his hard and narrow cot after waiting a long time in what he admitted was the probably foolish hope that Norna might come to him, Lomar dreamed. In his dream a huge and dun-grey rork stood a ways before and below him, its mask a bright yellow lineation; and it spoke to him in its hoarse, roaring and clicking voice. And what it said was:

"Come down . . . Come down . . . I kill! I kill!"

57

"These two are exempt," Old Guns said, hefting a matchlock in his hands, and indicating for Lomar to take the other from the table.

Lomar did, looking at it with curiosity. "What do you mean?"

"Well, I made them myself, and they aren't counted on the old man's roster. I mean that they are exempt from war. They are hunting weapons only, and I took my oath in blood upon them that they would never be aimed at any man no matter what. I did this before all the clans at the last powwow, some years back, and so everybody knows about it. That means that I can go anywhere with them at any time and no one will think I came to fight and I can pass safely. But it also means that if anyone wants to have at me, ever if a 'lock is pointed at me and primed and a lighted match at his touch hole, I am the same as unarmed. I can't use either of these even to defend myself. They're exempt, you see."

The match was made of a punk of wood and fungus, and burnt ill. Old Guns said that he might be able to make better, but preferred to keep to tradition. Besides, he had no desire to add to the arts of war as practiced too eagerly in the Wild land. One could usually tell where an armed enemy stood in the nighttime because his need often compelled him to whirl his match and fan it rapidly to keep it alive, and the sparks thrown off gave away his position. "To say nothing of the smell," he added, wryly.

"I make my own powder, too," he continued, "partly at least to keep from being blown up. But I tell them, when they ask me to make it for them, that it's only strong enough for hunt shot and couldn't kill a man. I use none of those big slugs that go for bullets here."

Powder "horn" (actually, a wooden flask) and shot bag were of traditional design, made by a clan craftsman who was of some small fame in such matters. On the bag was painted a rip, and the words—crude but quite legible—*I Bites;* and the horn was engraved with the figure of a rork and the legend, *Ware.*

Two long prongs folded from the heavy body of the matchlock to give it support when the 'lockman knelt to aim and fire; in order to do so from a standing position he would have needed three hands.

With the archaic instrument on his shoulder and powder and shot in place, Lomar felt like someone from

58

an ancient drama, the *First Men on Mars,* perhaps; or the *Revenge of Cleopatra.* "I'd wear a loincloth to match," he said, smiling, "if it weren't so cold." Old Guns did not smile, however, and made him repeat the rules for safety which he'd been told earlier. Finally, he allowed that it was safe for them to start out.

"What game are we after, by the way," Lomar asked. They were heading downhill and away from the sea, the camp above them sinking out of sight behind its dark walls. The snow had mostly melted, and once again the black color predominated. Black—the damp leaves underfoot, black—the boles of the naked trees, black—the moss growing thickly on them and on the black rocks.

"What we find is what we're after. Leapers, tree climbers, ant pigs, any of them are fit to eat, little though they may appeal to your Station-trained palate, boy. Daybats, maybe. Rips—I'd never eat a rip, though, believe me, there are those around who have, and glad to get them. . . . Rork?" He named the name hovering between them. "Not now; in Cold Time. They don't exactly hibernate, but almost. Slow, sluggish, weak, you know. I've known some of the young bucks to go out in Cold Time and drag back a young rork. Only a very, very young one, though the way they beat their chests about it, you'd think it was a great feat.

"The Tame Tocks, as you probably know, prize the claws for charms. And both they and the Wild men have this notion that the toes, if cooked, are good for *ambition,* as the Tame ones call it—the Wild ones are franker, they call it *rut.* If you've ever seen the things close up, it's not too hard to imagine why. Personally, I don't care one way or the other, but sometimes the creatures aren't quite dead when they drag them in; they butcher them alive, torture them. . . . I don't like to see that. . . ."

The ground was beginning to grow more level, the trees were larger. The nuts they had dropped lay all around and underfoot, inedible for men, and the arboreal creatures who lived on them had to descend to the ground to get them.

"They're a tough bunch of bumboes, your clan-kinsmen," Lomar said.

Old Guns nodded, shrugged. "Circumstances have made them so. You don't really know what their lives are like, you don't get a picture of it from my house. I live like a king. The old Mister himself doesn't eat better or sleep as warm and dry as we do. So you can imagine how the others live. And Mallardy is one of the richer clans, too! Every bite of food has to be wrestled out of this thin, rocky soil, and out of the sea . . . and the sea isn't exactly teeming, either. I'd say that a good half of them have never in their lives known what it is not to be hungry, have never once had a full belly. Think how it was in the early days, before they'd adapted, gotten acclimated—when redweed had become just a weed again and had no market value because there was no market. An empty sky over their heads and just the dirt beneath their feet. Waiting, waiting, waiting, for help that never came. Virtue must have died. It was dog eat dog, and root, hog, or die.

"So they fought like dogs and they rooted like hogs. And you see their children."

Lomar nodded. The air suddenly seemed colder. He shivered. "And so they hate us," he said, voice low.

"You have no idea how they hate you. *You,* I say. Not, *us.* Oh, Flinders hates me. But Flinders hates everyone. There is the ultimate Wild man for you, the Mister Flinders. But the others have accepted me. I've even been sounded out about joining them when they raid North."

Lomar glanced at his match, couldn't tell if it was still alive or not, shook it vigorously till it glowed up and threw sparks. He tried to form a map in his mind of the territories of the clans from the bits of information gotten at the haphazard and only vaguely remembered. Hannit and Haggar and Crame. Dominis, Nimmai, Boylston, Owelly. . . . He ran out of names, could form no picture.

"North? Whose camp lies north of here?" he asked.

Old Guns slowly blew out his breath, watched it misting in the morning air. "Yours does," he said, at last. "The Station."

The game bag on the way back contained a tree climber and two leapers. They had given the offals to a scrannel, ragged hag who had appeared from nowhere; Lomar, insomuch as he thought of it at all, thought that she might well intend to eat them all raw.

60

For perhaps the hundredth time he asked, "But you can't be serious?"

His host shrugged. "Have it your own way, then," he muttered.

"No—I mean, *they* can't be serious! . . . *can* they? It's madness—"

Old Guns sighed and waggled his head. "Of course it is. Isn't all war madness? And the Wild men are all at least a little mad and some of them, Florus Flinders, for example, are more than a little mad. No so long ago he and Haggar raided into Nimmai's Camp. They were repulsed. He had at least some sort of a claim against Nimmai, but then he raided Owelly, and he had no claim at all against Owelly. What was his reason? He was hungry. Owelly had food and Flinders didn't. *Thou shalt want ere I shall want.* Isn't that a sort of insanity?"

The grievances of the Wild Tocks against the Guild were deep and bitter and old. The Guild had committed no new, specific act to antagonize them lately—but lately they had found a focus for their discontent in Flinders. The Guild was rich, they were poor. How had the Guild become rich? By taking redwing cheap and selling it dear. Therefore the riches of the Guild rightfully belonged to the Tocks. The Guild Station had food, it had clothing. Why should others go naked, cold, unshod? It had weapons, too.

It had guns.

"But . . . but . . . listen. They think of those weapons as booty to plunder for. Don't they realize that they are capable of being used against them, as well as by them?"

Ran Lomar, Old Guns said, was arguing rationally. By this time he should have learned that men are not always moved to act rationally. Had Lomar, with all his rational arguments, been able to persuade any of the Guildsmen? No, not one. And if sophisticated, educated, far-traveled and civilized folk could not be swayed by logic and sense, then what was to be expected from those who had lived for generations on the thin edge of barbarism? going nowhere, learning nothing, minds dulled by parochialism, hunger, bitterness, and a form of pride so perverted that it scarcely deserved the name.

A solitary daybat broke the solitude of the sky. Quickly, automatically, Old Guns glanced at it, fingers moving for his matchlock. Then his glance dropped away, and his fingers. The swooping, fluttering, erratic flight made it a bad target. The mournful cry of the creature fell upon their ears, distant and thin. Then it vanished.

"You've heard or read about a telescope, boy? An archaic form of farseer? If you looked through the right end—it was only fitted for one eye—then, of course, small things seemed large. But if you looked through the opposite end, the wrong end, then even large things seemed small. Now—you and the Wild men are looking through opposite ends. You see the situation as a handful of Tocks against the teeming Galaxy. And they see it as thousands of Tocks against a handful of Guildsmen. Ah . . . Don't they realize the numbers and the power of the world Outside? No. They don't. How could they? None of them have ever been Outside. They've seen no more than the Station. Once every five years comes one single ship. You can talk to them till your teeth ache, as I've done, as I've done; it's no use. Academically they may acknowledge that a few, a very few, other worlds may be inhabited besides this one and Old Earth.

"But they can't conceive that they are inhabited any more thickly than this world is. The Q Ship is not a war ship, they know that much. They think its schedule is a sort of act of nature: It couldn't return in less than five years any more than the sun can rise or set in less than its allotted time. So they figure: suppose they attack the Station. Conquer they must. The Q comes. Perhaps they conquer the Q. Even if they don't, it would be years before it returns. By that time they are impregnable. Besides, do they not control all the redwing in the Universe? Guild will have to make terms. . . . That's how it looks to them. That's how it looks."

They plodded along in silence. A thousand thoughts fleeted through Lomar's mind. Should he leave now and warn the Station? No—impossible—the boat wouldn't be back for weeks. A surprise attack might possibly succeed. Suddenly, sickeningly, he realized that it might very possibly succeed! And even if he should get up North in time, would he be believed? He knew that he would not, he could not, never in a million years convince any of them that such a danger existed. What, then? Make his own escape? Persuade Lindel and perhaps a few Tame Tocks—build a raft (his own past fantasies now return-

62

ing, more vigorous than before)—try and make a landfall on another continent or island?

Supposing, and it was not too healthy a supposition—this to succeed—what then? Live like the first generation of the forefathers of the Tocks, with the prospect of their children falling into a similar degeneration?

His thoughts went around and round, and the wind grew cold against his shoulders.

"When—" His voice came out low and thick, and he struggled to clear his throat. "When do they plan this attack?"

"Oh," said Old Guns, almost indifferently, "they have no plans. Not yet. It's still just talk, just firestone talk. But it's a talk that begins to grow louder. Maybe the main thing keeping it down—" He stopped, frowned; shook his head. "—so far, is that it is known to be Flinders' idea. No one likes Flinders. No one trusts . . ." Again he stopped, his voice fading off, again he frowned.

He stopped. "Speak of the devil," he muttered. "I could swear I heard Flinders' voice—be quiet," he said abruptly. Lomar, who had said nothing, continued to say nothing. They stood in their steps, listening. At first Lomar could hear nothing but the occasional slight *pit-pit-pit* of the again-falling snowflakes against the tree behind him. Then the wind changed. Then he heard voices. He could not tell how many, but above them on the changeable wind, now sharp, now gone, now fading, falling, rising—one voice: loud, loud, loud.

"It *is* Flinders. What's he—Ranny! Remember, now! These 'locks are exempt! Don't load, don't prime, certainly don't fire, and if you want us all to live, *don't even point!*"

Before Ran could reply he saw the band of men coming through the woods ahead of them. And, at the same moment, they were seen. Several of Flinders' men dropped at once to the one-knee position, flipping out the supports for their 'locks and blowing on their matches.

"Covered!" cried Flinders, his bristly face splitting into an unpleasant grin. "Ye's be covered, says!"

"We know it," Old Guns answered, coming on. "You know me, Mister. I use no tricks."

The clan chief lifted his upper lip. "Says, 'I use no tricks.' Use any, an' we puts bullets in ye. If ye doesn't fear bullets—" his whole mouth expressed his glee and

63

his triumph, "—then we has what'll makes ye fear!" His men guffawed. "Strip! Come up. Come up."

Flinders' heir-son, an ungrizzled version of his unlovely sire, came forward. And with him, hands bound and feet hobbled, defiantly tossing back her long black hair, was Norna.

Old Guns groaned, whispered her name. "Sathy? Is she—is your mother—? Child—?"

It was sudden.

He had put out his arms toward his daughter, forgetting the matchlock lying flat on his shoulder. It slipped, he reached for it quickly, two guns roared, Norna screamed, Lomar cried out, men shouted, and Old Guns pitched forward and collapsed.

Flinders shouted, cursed. "A ransom gone!" he cried. "Oh, ye sluts' gets, ye rorks' eggs! What'll he fetch, dead?" He kicked at the still-kneeling, openmouthed 'locksmen, and they cringed and cowered. Norna screamed, ran forward, tripped on her hobbles, was saved from falling by Strip's quick hand. And Lomar, unbelieving, incredulous, knelt awkwardly and tried to move the bleeding form of his host. But the Mister Flinders had been right.

Old Guns was dead.

Apparently, though, it was intended that he should fetch at least enough, dead, to justify taking the body along. At first a line of bright red on the trampled snow marked his trail. But it grew colder, colder, and presently the blood congealed. Norna wept and wailed as she was tugged along; and Lomar, tied and hobbled, too, trudged along, numbly behind her.

To right and to left a file of matchlockmen held them in guard as they marched on through the thin snow masking parts of the black-mossed landscape, their matches and their breath smoking in the cold grey air.

CHAPTER FOUR

By and by the Mister Flinders' face began to assume its normal coloring—red and purple cheeks, yellow patches around the eyes, putty grey at the porous nose, the drooping lips a lead-blue—and he rubbed the quills of his jowls with great satisfaction.

"Not a bad day's jobby, Strip," he said.

"No, Dad. We's gots a pair more 'lock, a hee!" snickered the heir-son.

"Piss," said his dad, succinctly, waving his furry paws. "We's gots more'n that, says. Looks—" He began to count off. "Gots the pretty piecey there," indicating Norna, and adding the warning, "None's to plug her, hears? Jun Mallardy s'll pay me a three pair o' 'lock, besides pikes and hacks and powder and bullets—mm, and eats, too! —for her. So she be's not to be plugged by any dirty egg of a rork. *Hears!* Jun'll want she whole. Firsts. And what seconds, says? Why, seconds be's the stiff one, there. Old woman Sathy s'll gi' alls in her house for her man, else he's feeds the rorks. It be's good cold, and he's to keep till she do. So, seconds. And what's thirds? Strip, says, what's thirds?"

Strip gaped, unable to think what "thirds" might be.

"Why, ye leaper's cod," his father spat in disgust. "What's in ye head? Boiled tata-meal? Thirds is the Guild turd, tripsing over his feets, there! Ah, hoy, what a ransom we s'll gets for him, hey? Name it! Name it? Men—?"

All the clansmen began speaking at once.

"Guns! Guns and gun-makins!"

"Bullets!"

"Sulphur!"

"Metal!"

"*Guild's* guns!"

"Eats!"

The Mister Flinders nodded, grinned, his tiny, shrewd, gummy little eyes almost swallowed up in the yellow patches of skin, grinned and nodded. "All o' thems," he said, paused to hawk phlegm and spit. "All o' thems, and more, says."

His vassals could scarce conceive of this. *"More?"* they cried, astonished.

Their lord nodded again, rubbed his hands and scratched his arm-pit. "Thinks. How many times be's a Guildsman catched for ransom? They thinks themselves, oh, hoy, so big, hey? Alls for them, and for us, whats? Piss and scrapins. Soft, they be's, softer than a woman's prettyplace. Squeeze, an' they weeps. Well, the rorks' eggs s'll be squeezed for this one. And they s'll pay.

Oh . . ." His voice grew low and grim, "how they s'll pay . . ."

Lomar, wincing at the tightness of his bonds, had his doubts that he and his freedom would be valued all that much. Many at the Station would be glad to have seen the last of him, no doubt. But he thought he might depend somewhat on the favor of Tan Carlo Harb, the Station Officer. And others, Lindel's father, for example, would be well-disposed toward him. To be sure there was no precedent for ransoming a Guildsman kidnapped by Wild Tocks. But it was not likely to happen often. And if they failed (resolutely, he put out of his mind all thoughts of what his captors might do if the Guild Station failed to pay ransom) they would damage their own precious image at least as much as if they paid.

There was nothing that he could do about it now, anyway.

It was black night before they paused, their shelter being a cave in the now steadily rising hills, where a fire burned in welcome. Guards were there, and food. Little enough food, although the Mister Flinders saw that the prisoners drew an even share.

"He's not to be stripped, nor her," warned the chief. "Her, because Mallardy's heir-son be's not to like it. And I wants him on our side, hears? The old Mister's sure to die soon. Gots gut, Jun. And the Guild's egg's not be stripped, either. They be's puny and I doesn't wants him sickening or dead."

His solicitude extended even to seeing that their bonds were removed. He urged them to rub their wrists and ankles to restore circulation, and he kicked two men away from the firestone to make room for them. Guards were in the narrow passage between the cold and blackness outside and the great main cavern. No roof was visible in the darkness relieved only by the leaping flames. Now and then someone got up and relieved himself, noisily, or simply rolled over and went to sleep . . . usually more noisily.

At length the Mister Flinders belched, followed the casual custom of his crew, and prepared himself for rest. "Be's no way out the back," he said to Ran and Norna. "Looks, if you likes." And in another moment his phlegmy snore joined the chorus. Ran's last waking memory was of Norna sitting up, arms around her knees, hair falling over the sides of her tear-stained face, looking into the dying fire.

The fire revived in the morning, briefly. Stale-tasting melted snow was drunk from a dirty bowl, and for food everyone had a handful of dried . . . something. Ran did not care to speculate. Insofar as the foul-looking stuff had any taste at all, it tasted bad. The bladder brigade held its usual drill, and this time Ran, with a mental shrug, joined them; delicately (and uniquely) turning his back. The bonds were replaced, and then they were all off on march again.

His shoes were stout and his legs were strong, but even on his trip with Rango (Rango! What would the Tame Tocks do, and what would be done to them, if there should be an attack upon the Station?) he had not been forced to such a pace. The double files did not falter for his stumbling. One man on each side grasped him with an arm that was all bone and sinew, and helped him to keep up. Norna matched them step for step, her eyes seldom leaving her father's body, born along on a crude litter of poles and ropes, his arms and legs rigid and stiff.

Lomar had lost track of the time. Pia Sol was now and then visible, a faded red globe, in the pearl-grey, dove-grey, lead-grey skies; now and then it vanished with the changing shades and the inconstant snows. So he had no notion of how far they had come when—not a shout, not even his captors had breath to spare for that—a union of voices roused his drooping head.

Someone poked him in the ribs with the butt end of a pike and, his attention secured, pointed the pike ahead and to the left. A great cairn of boulders stood a ways above the path. "What is it?" he asked, stupidly, tongue thick and mouth foul, lungs biting with the freezing air.

"That be's the mark," said the pikeman. "Flinders' Country now . . . and minds you knows it, pogue! Him as watches—" he gestured more particularly, as if setting down the pikestaff, "—forgot." A blur of yellow and white and three black holes met his eyes and vanished as he was jerked along. Suddenly his head cleared and the memory focused: it was a human, chinless skull which perched there atop the cairn, mantled with snow.

Here and there an apronful of ground bore, where the winds had blown away the snow, the marks of cultivation.

From such scanty bits and pockets of soil did the Flinder folk tear their frugal food . . . when they did not tea it from the mouths of other clans. The double files be came a single file, snaking its way along the slope an over the crest of the hills—and then something between sigh and a groan arose, and even Lomar, head snappe back, said, "*Oh* . . ."

A mass of black and naked rock, broken, jagged splotched with snow, thrust itself up from the risin ground. And up. And up . . .

And up . . .

It was not quite a mountain.

"Flinders Crag," said the pikeman. He grimaced, swal lowed.

"Home," said the pikeman.

He never did see the camp from below, never knew h was coming to it until they were almost there. For sud denly there was no longer the gaunt rock all about him and once again nothing but the sky. Nothing but the sky And then another turn, this one down, and the women came forth from the meager fortress to greet them.

The greeting was in silence at first. When the Miste said, "Alls 'live," the women burst into sound and mo tion, even his aged mother throwing up her match-thir arms and lifting her claws of feet as she tripped a few steps in dreadful parody of what had once— God knev how very long ago!—been a dance. But the frolic wa short, the air was cold, and after a few formal, ritua exercises pikemen and 'lockmen were dismissed to do as they pleased. Which, as Lomar gathered from the coarse jocose comments, was to have rough, brief joy of thei wives and then to sit about their firestones and talk an scratch themselves and dream of food and plunder.

Victor, chieftain on his own soil, the Mister Flinder was able to recall and to extend what fragments of cour tesy he still retained of what custom demanded. The captives—there was no prison keep, for that matter— were his guests. Their hands and legs were freed. The camp's gate was guarded . . . and, besides, where, in thi wilderness of rock and snow, where could they go? A daughter and a younger son were detailed to keep watch upon them. To Norna was accorded the question able honor of sharing the old mother's bed of sour rags and for Lomar a skin was spread not too far from the fire.

"I am so very sorry," he said to Norna, the first chance they had a free moment together from the hordes of clansmen who coursed through the house to see the captives and revel in the thought that they might themselves gain some share in their ransom.

She bent her head lower for a moment, then looked up at him. "He's been put in the powder magazine," she said. "It's dry . . . they said they couldn't gives any cover for him . . . but I thinks he doesn't need none now."

He nodded, and murmured something of her father's love for the Wild country, and his desire to be buried there, and she wept a moment. Then there was another trample of feet and a loud burst of voices, she turned away, and when next he looked her way she was proud and calm.

The Mister Flinders was much concerned with what his ransom messages should contain, and how they were to be composed. Those to Jun Mallardy and Sathy gave the lesser concern; truce-men from that clan might be expected by and by. But how to send word to the Guild Station? And what was that word to be? The art of writing was an aspect of the arcane which the Mister had never concerned himself with, but he did have one man who was popularly supposed to be versed in the crafts of reading and writing. Either he had not mastered them well at the start or years of being out of practice had rusted his familiarity with them; or perhaps he was shy of displaying his talents; at any rate he was long in coming, and his lord cursed him roundly when he appeared.

The sage drooped and shrugged and wiped his nose on his ragged sleeve. Finally the storm of wrath abated, and he was allowed to sit at the table-board, from the surface of which as much dirt and grease was rubbed—or smeared —as possible (with the same sleeve). He spread out some yellowed, smudgy bits of paper, spit into the bit of pottery which served as inkwell, trimmed himself a reed pen rather clumsily, squared his elbows, and by the set of his face announced himself ready for business.

The matter was not one to be settled in one evening, however. Clearly, the Mister was in an agony lest he should ask too little or ask too much. And finally he declared (and was supported by his followers, crowding around the unhappy scribe who had been setting down the

words letter by slow and awkward letter) that he ha
"gots to thinks more" about it, first.

Muck-Hell, yes!

He thought about it several days, during whch Ran an
Norna, together or alone, wandered as they wishe
about the dirty camp. Its walls were in poor conditior
but no one worried about that, for the Crag itself wa
wall enough, and more. Lomar observed with some amuse
ment that the guards seemed as much concerned with safe
guarding Norna's virtue as preventing their escape.

The thought that leaped first into his mind, then, o
that third or fourth night, when he awoke to find he
hand over his mouth and her hair brushing his face, wa
that she had decided to part with that virtue. This hope
however, did not deceive him too long. A faint, dull glov
from the fire on the hearthstone in the middle of the roor
—carelessly, typically, not banked—did not revea
much. But it was enough to show that Tig Flinders, th
younger son and supposed guard, had left his post an
taken his sleeping skin with him. Scraps of rough-laughin
gossip came to his mind; the boy had had some amou
of his own going and evidently concluded not to le
Lomar's presence interfere with it any longer. As for hi
sister, a vigorous soprano snore indicated that neither he
guard duties nor her deviated septum was keeping he
from sound sleep.

Lomar rose from his own pelt—Norna indicated, wit
a gesture, that he was to take it with him, as she was tak
ing hers—and, hand in hand, they tiptoed out of th
room. The door gave him pause, for it had creaked lustil
whenever it was opened. This had not escaped the girl'
attention, though. She had taken a fish-oil lamp from th
table in passing, now she poured its contents over th
hinges, they waited a moment or two for the stinkin
fluid to penetrate . . . then they lifted up the heavy bean
which barred the door, and passed silently into the nigh

There were, indeed, places on Old Earth, thousand
and thousands of square leagues, parts of which Ran ha
visited, that saw lower temperatures and deeper snow
than any place in Tockland South. But on his visits ther
he had been dressed against the cold in heated clothes,
flick of his thumb not even needed, for the tiny thermo
stats were geared to the immediate needs of his ow

70

body. Furthermore, he had gone there in much company, and for larks—skiing, bobsledding—sometimes for no more than a snowball fight: so little did they make of time and distance there. Sooner or later, of course, he'd tired of it all, the enforecd comradeship, obligatory competitions, the whole business . . .

But never had he felt the cold as now, groping his way down the narrow path through the Crag, slippery with snow, nothing but ordinary winter clothing and the worn sleeping skin to protect him. There was no light, not even starlight, for the clouds obscured it, and they dared make none; not knowing if their escape might be discovered any minute.

They were alone, just the two of them. And this time it was no lark.

It was almost dawn before they reached the foot of the Crag. He could not be sure, reflecting on it afterwards, if he had actually heard anything, or if he had only turned and looked up instinctively. It had seemed to him that there had been a faint shout . . . but it might have had no origin outside his mind. Nor was he ever certain of what he saw—if he had seen anything, for Norna had neither seen nor heard. But he was sure, then, that following the sound, he had seen a faint and scattered light far, far above.

A light which might have been that of someone whirling a stick of match-punk.

But it might have only been his imagination, or retinal strain aggravated by peering through the dangerous darkness.

Norna, when it did grow light, said that there was no point to running until they found flatter or at least more gentle ground—free from snow if possible. They might stumble among the rocks and any injury could easily prove fatal . . . how far could he carry her, or she, him? They might come to regard recapture as a blessing. He commended her common sense, proceeded thereafter at a safer and a less exhausting pace.

It was Norna, too, who had given thought to provisons, had stolen food from the Mister's scanty larder, and carried a coal of fire in a shell wrapped in mud and moss (from time to time refreshing it with what dry fungus they found on route); it was Norna who pointed out

71

certain shrubs whose wood burned without smoke—it was too soon to pause to build a fire, but the shell, passed from hand to hand, kept their fingers warm. Alone, he realized, he would have stood little chance of making good his escape. It remained to be seen how good their chances were, together.

"Shall we try for the shore?" he asked.

She shook her head. "No path keeps for long there." Sooner, rather than later, the cliffs would force them back inland. No easy route was open to them. Haggar's lands were nearest, but Haggar was an open ally of Flinders, had accompanied him on his last raid; they dared not be seen by him or his people. But if they cut across the unoccupied corner of his land they would find themselves on Owelly's grounds, and close by—for the corner was a narrow one—Nimmai's territory marched, too. Either Mister was bound to afford them sanctuary, or to conduct them to whatever place would.

"And they doesn't love Flinders, neither one."

So she reasoned, and reasoned well enough. But evidently Flinders had reasoned the same, for about mid-morning she cried out. Before he could so much as speak, she had seized his arm and, together, they turned in their tracks and darted back into the woods from which they had just emerged. There, safe for the moment from observation, they gazed at the ridge for which they had been making.

A line of tiny black figures climbed along it in double file.

"Flinders . . ." Lomar breathed.

"Maybe. Or maybe Haggar. If it's Haggar, Flinders has alerted him. But I thinks it's likelier Flinders, for if he asks Haggar to help him, he musts share ransom with him. Flinders wishen'ts to do that, you know, Ranny."

His hand felt for his farseer, but of course it was not there. The orders that he should not be stripped had protected it, but he had taken it off when he slept, the first night, thrusting it into a niche in the wall when he hoped that Tig was not awake to see. It had remained there so far as he knew.

So far as he knew! For if Tig knew, if Tig had revealed it, if any of them had figured out how to work it, then Lomar and Norna were in worse plight than they had thought. So, slowly, he told her. She sighed.

"Let's hopes they hasn't got it, or the use of it. But we can't chance it. We must keeps to the woods, much as we can, even though—" her voice faltered, and, for the first time, he saw something . . . fear? . . . not quite . . despair? . . . not yet. . . . Dismay.

"Norna? 'Even though—'? Tell me."

She looked directly into his eyes, and said, "Even though it takes us into Rorkland."

An involuntary, startled *"Oh!"* escaped him. He said to himself that it was the cold which made him shudder. He repeated to himself that the old records must be considered more reputable and authentic than latter-day legends, present Station personnel being too indifferent and both Wild Tocks and Tame too ignorant to be believed. And yet, once again, without his willing it, up from the depths of his mind and soul, came that *"Oh!"* bursting from his stiffened lips.

And again, he shuddered.

Norna said, "It's luck that Cold Time's here. The orks will be changing their skins."

"Yes, I know," he muttered, swinging his arms to keep warm. It *was* luck. All agreed that in Cold Time the ork were sluggish, not dangerous. . . . Or, at any rate, not so dangerous. Didn't even the Tame Tocks, whose corrupted vocabulary scarcely included the word or concept of "Courage"—didn't even they venture into Rorkland during Cold Time? Yes, they did. Of course they did.

But they did so in full force, often accompanied by armed Station personnel. They did not do so alone, or u pair, and with no defenses save their own hands and feet and native wit. No. . . .

It was useless for him to pretend that he was unafraid. The rorks were too different, vastly much too different, and the encouraging reports too long ago and the terrifying ones too recent, for him not to fear. Better the devil one knew. He turned to her, to tell her that it was best that they return. And she, still looking directly at him, said, "I won't be too afraid, because you re with me."

His open mouth closed upon his counsel of retreat. 'an Carlo Harb, for whatsoever reasons (and Lomar new that the reasons would be neither all good nor all ad), would certainly give *something* to effect his man's

release, not the things that Flinders wanted, of course
but enough, disguised as "presents for assistance" or
some such face-saving device. And Flinders, faced with
take-it-or-leave-it, and a boatload of . . . what? . . .
sulphur, some sulphur could certainly be spared, coarse
food (it would be delicate to Flinders), enough scrap
metal for a few pair of matchlocks, and clothes worn
slightly enough to be allowed him instead of a favored
Tame Tock servant, but so slightly that he'd never know
the difference . . . what else? . . . outmoded furniture
perhaps . . . Flinders would settle for that, and return
Ran Lomar (*Three*, but with an assimilated rating of
seven) with his head and testicles intact. He would
hardly dare do otherwise. Yet.

But what about Norna? The SO's tastes were not in
clined towards women. *They count her as a Tock, damn
them*, her father—now stiff and cold in the Mister
Flinders' powder shed—had said. Not even as a half
breed. New blood or not, no, Harb would give nothing
at all for her. Certainly not if he heard (as he must)
that the Mister Mallardy's heir-son was willing to ransom
her. If he was.

"You don't fancy Jun, do you?" Lomar asked.

Her face sickened a bit. Perhaps she had followed
his train of thought. "He's always being after me," she
said, low-voiced. "While my old dad was there, I could
says No. But he's be glad to ransom me. And if he pays
he takes me." She added no further word of elabora
tion, but her face told her feelings, clear enough.

"Well, he won't," said Ran. He took her cold, cold
hands in his. "We'll skirt through Rorkland till we can
cut back into friendly soil again. Come on." She didn't
move. "Come on," he repeated, giving her arm a tug
"let's get going."

He turned once to peer through the covering trees
Had they been discovered? or their location even
suspected?

But the last of the double-file of tiny figures was toil
ing over the crest of the distant ridge, heading away
from them. Pursuit seemed lost, for now.

It did not remain lost forever. Late that afternoon
climbing a wooded hill, he yielded to an impulse several
minutes in the growing, and shinned up the mossy side

f a slant tree. Norna said that a hollow place between
ιe ground and the massy roots, made large by the
εe's gradual lean towards one side, would be of good
se for a small, smokeless fire of *teen*-wood. But a sud-
εn hiss from above put an end to her preparations,
nd brought her quickly up the tree to just below him.
[e pointed.

At first she could see nothing; then, following his hand,
far off she saw a black dot passing across a clearing
ι the distance. His hand moved, pointed, moved, pointed,
ιoved . . .

. . . pointed. And every place where the index finger
ιdicated showed another black dot. Moving forward
:eadily, in a thin and drawn-out line. It could only be
ιen. And the men could only be seeking . . . them.

Down on the ground again, they allowed themselves
ιe small, brief comfort of warming their hands on the
ny and just lighted fire. Then they kicked snow over it,
nd were off. The pursuers were moving at a diagonal.
t was not possible to say just how long the line was,
ιe background landscape was too broken and in places
ɔo wooded to allow for that. Nor could they calculate
ither how many people were following, and extrapolate
:om that. It could only be certain that more than armed
ιen were involved, for neither Flinders nor Haggar, nor
ˀlinders *and* Haggar, had enough pike or 'lockmen to
ccount for even the number they had seen.

All that Ran and Norna knew was enough to tell them
hat if they intended to make as certain as they could
f not meeting those who were scouting the snows in
hat diagonal line which moved athwart their intended
»ath, it was impossible merely to "skirt through Rork-
ιnd." They would have to thrust more deeply into that
orbidden region. To go directly ahead was no less im-
»ossible than to go directly behind. They would have to
ιove at a diagonal of their own, so plotted, and at
uch a speed that they would not only not be over-
aken but would eventually be able to make an angle
nd turn the flank of the pursuers' line. Possibly the
»urpose of the diagonal was for that line to move in a
ull circle, like the hand of a clock, and scan every
ɔod and plot within the great circle.

And whether within that circle they found the fugitives or not, given sufficient time, there they must surely find their spoor.

Ran and Norna faced each other, clasped hands for a moment, and then turned and fled down the long slope of the hill.

Fortunately, Pia Sol had come out from the concealing clouds long enough for them to make a more accurate picture of their location, approximate though it could only be; and hence they were fairly sure of their direction.

All that long afternoon they went on without stopping, and it was when Ran was about to confess his inability to proceed, that she pointed out to him the landmark which was Tiggy's Hill. No boundary commission had ever demarcated where Wild Tockland left off and South Rorkland began. But Tiggy's Hill, with its unmistakable double peak and wide col, was without doubt part of the latter. Thoughts of danger, however, were not in his mind. Indeed, it was not his mind at all, but his cold and aching body which now answered her.

"I can't make it . . ."

"You gots to!" In her urgency and distress she fell into the deeper Wild Tock dialect which the constant example of her father's speech had previously kept her from when talking to Lomar. "Ranny! We gots to makes Tiggy's Hill before it darks! There be's sorts of houses there, to keep the snows and winds and the freezy mists off us. If we doesn't gets there, we s'll die before morning. Ranny!"

She pulled one of his arms around her, and led him off. At a walk, at a stumbling trot, at a plodding gait they went on. He protested and almost wept when she insisted that they round the foot of the hill and ascend by the farther side to prevent being seen against its often treeless slopes, but she kept them going. By coaxing, by cajolery, by singing songs, by threats, by all of a score of different means, she kept them going. Nor did she forget to change sides at frequent intervals, so that each could thrust a right hand and then a left inside their own clothing to warm it and keep it from frostbite.

Insensibly, it darkened. He lost track of everything except a need to pick a foot up, move it, put it down, pick up the other one, put it down. His face was no quite yet so numb that he did not feel the sting of the now and rain which, alternately, beat upon it. He heard . voice—somewhere—close—croaking, "Let me alone . . alone . . ." And finally she did. His arm, released, ell heavily, and he fell with it.

Sprawling, he was long in realizing that the ground eneath was dry, that the whip and lash of rain and now had ceased. Now he observed the sudden flicker of . fire, and all his flesh began to sting. They had made he sanctuary of Tiggy's Hill, and were, for at least the noment, safe in the rough shelter of the redwing gath- rers.

"It's luck there's wood," she said, as much to her- elf as to him. He couldn't hear her next words although er lips moved, and then, recalling her father's grace at neals, realized that she was not speaking to him.

When she had stopped and was feeding another piece f wood to the small fire, he asked, "Isn't this place sed?"

She shrugged. "If nobody was here when we came, obody's likely to come before we go . . . if we doesn't tay too long."

Presently they were warmed enough to eat the last of heir little store of food, and then, to sleep. He did not now what the time might be when he awoke, stiff, ching, a sharp raw pain somewhere inside of him be- ween his back and his lungs. A dull grey light came in rough the doorless opening at the other end of the helter, and he saw Norna scratching in the dirt with a tick.

"I'm not much use to you," he said, after a moment.

She looked up, surprised. There was a streak of char n one side of her face, from brushing her hair back. I'd be afraid . . . alone," she said. Then—"Look." He at, cross-legged, beside her, and watched as she ex- lained her drawings. If they were to head back south, lmost all of *this* area—she covered it with her palm— as certain to be unsafe. As for the rest—

"As for the rest?" he prompted her, when she fell lent.

Her explanation silenced him, as well. She was no onger certain that, her father dead, any part of Wild 'ockland was now safe for her. She could not really e sure that Flinders would not have corrupted the other

77

Misters with offers of a share in Lomar's ransom, with talk of unity against the interloping Guild.

"But . . . wouldn't you be safe at least in Mallardy' Camp? Your own camp?"

"Least safe, there. You know . . . Jun . . ."

He did not know Jun well, but he knew Jun well enough. And the sick look once again on her face a she mentioned his name decided him. He looked at th crude map scratched into the earthen floor.

"Could we live off the land—find enough to eat—if w cut north and try to make it to the Guild Station?"

She said, "We maybe could."

"And get through before Cold Time is over and th rorks really begin to stir?"

She said, "We maybe could."

He scrambled to his feet. "Then let's get going."

She took an ember from the fire and cased it an wrapped it and kicked dirt over what was left. "I'r ready," she said. They went down, as they had come up the far side of the hill. Nothing moved as far as ey could reach, not even a daybat fluttered against the lead en sky. All seemed cold. All seemed dead. Far behin them, against a snow-free black hill, lay a patch of some thing thin and white. It might have been smoke. It migh have been mist.

"Well, Ranny," he said aloud, but to himself, "yo wanted to explore the continent. And now you're damne well going to."

They moved north, into the dread heart of Rorkland.

Sometimes their drink was snow, sometimes when i melted they stooped and drank from the puddles, some times they had to break a film of ice and suck the shat tered shards. Now and then they were able to brin down small game with rocks. Occasionally a rip was see slinking away, but offered no menace beyond the mer unease caused by its presence. Certain places Norna le him around rather than across, indicating by finger o lips and waggling hand that it was the sort of place rork preferred to nest in. Here and there they found a tre around whose base a few withered fruits still lay, thei usually astringent flesh nipped by the frost into edibility For the first time in his life Lomar became familiar wit hunger. He remembered, ruefully, the comment of Ol

78

Guns that this was the constant condition of many of the Wild Tocks.

Periodically he and Norna scouted the landscape (the brown of withered redwing the predominant color motif now) for signs of pursuit. They saw no files of men, no mists that they were not sure *were* mists.

They had been awhile on their way, guiding themselves by the infrequent sun alone, when they began to feel that they were being followed. Or, perhaps, not so much followed, as observed. They heard an occasional faint noise when there was no wind, no sign of any animal. Now and then they saw something flicker out of the corner of an eye. These things did not happen often. But they continued to happen. And once he chanced to turn quickly around, prompted by nothing he was able to name, to see something vanish in that instant over the crest of a not too distant hill. Something too large for any animal they knew of . . . something too small for a rork.

"What do you think, Norna?" he asked. "Any of Flinders' men?"

She was emphatic that it was not. Flinders or any of his had no notion of subtlety. They would have been set upon long before this. No . . . not Flinders. Not any of the Wild Tocks. Had she any idea at all what it might be? No. She had none. They concluded that whatever it was—assuming there to be an actual It and not a mere series of naturally explainable and insignificant coincidences magnified by their nerves and imaginations—it was not dangerous; had it been capable of harming them, it would already have done so.

That night they slept in a cave on a downward slope of land. He was awakened by an internal pressure, and made his way silently past her sleeping form to the mouth of the cavern. His astonished and marvelling cry brought her to his side in a second.

"The city!" she cried. "The city of the rorks!"

Far, far ahead and far, far below, near the horizon, it lay, shimmering and flickering with constant light, myriads of lights in an infinite variety of colors, spread out for a great space. It could not be an aurora, could not appear toward the center of the landmass and not at either extremity of it; an aurora capped and cloaked the sky, it did not appear as points of light upon the ground.

The appearance utterly baffled him, he did not know what to say.

Norna did, though, or thought she did. There was no doubt in her mind, only dismay. This was certainly the city of the rorks. They would have to go very far from the direct route which they intended in order to avoid it. But he would not agree.

"Whatever it is," he said, "it can't have anything to do with rorks. Did anyone ever see rorks there? Did anyone ever see anything at all there in the daytime? No. There, you see . . . And even if it should have something to do with them, there is no reason to think that they are more dangerous there—at this time—than anywhere else. We don't dare, I think, go that far out of our way to avoid it. We cannot spare the time. We don't dare get caught here when the winter ends."

Reluctantly, she conceded his point. But . . . she wanted to know . . . if the lights did not indicate a habitation of rorks . . . what then?

He could only theorize. Perhaps, anciently, before the arrival of man on the planet, there had been a settlement by another race. Perhaps—presumably—this race had died off or simply moved elsewhere. It was hardly likely that if any members of it remained that nothing should have been seen, heard, or otherwise known of them all these centuries. He theorized that the lights, powered by an unknown source, continued to burn eternally; "eternally" in comparative terms, for even the once eternal pyramids, undermined by the irrigation of the Egyptian desert, had eventually crumbled into rubble. But Norna, who had never heard of Egypt or of pyramids, shook her head in incomprehension. The only argument that weighed at all with her was that the rorks were likely to be as sluggish among the lights as those anywhere else.

While Cold Time lasted.

The so-called Plain of Lights was dull and blear enough in the daytime, stretching flatly on ahead. There was no sign of a city, and indeed it differed, aside from its flatness, from the rest of the country they had passed through, chiefly in the type of vegetation. Vaguely, the plant forms reminded him of those still surviving in the World Park at what was once called the Mountains of the

Moon in Africa, on Old Earth. Predominating over every other kind of flora were fleshy stalks, leafless, branchless, bearing only. . . . He hesitated how to describe them. Bulbs? Nodes? Cones? They still had some food with them, but it was not much.

Gingerly, he tore off one of the protuberances and touched it to his tongue. It tasted faintly bitter, and he threw it away. Later, perhaps, if their food gave out and could not be replenished, if starvation menaced them directly, they might be obliged to risk poisoning or illness: try the strange fruit (if fruit it was) raw or baked. . . . But not now and not yet.

As the day went on with no sign of any city, no sign of any landmark, no sign of either observation or pursuit, senses dulled by the monotony of the landscape, they began to walk more slowly. And, finally, by mutual consent some while yet before sunset, they curled up and went to sleep, Ran's stolen pelt beneath them, Norna's over them.

It was deep dusk when they awoke and stretched. There was no sense in trying to travel by night, but they thought to look for water before settling down for further sleep. On their feet, peering through the twilight, they saw the last rays of Pia Sol dwindle behind the horizon. And then, suddenly and without warning, it happened.

One moment a faint tinge of sunset was at the edge of the sky. The next moment it had vanished. For scarcely a second the world was utterly dark. And then, as if someone had touched a master switch, the world sprang into light, into a blaze of brilliant and fantastically variegated colors. They both cried out, turned and turned to see around them. Everywhere, the same thing. Every one of the strange plants was pulsing and glowing with the light of its nodes; each one displaying one general class of color, but each color varying within its type. Here one saw orange shading into pink, pink into rose, rose into scarlet, scarlet into crimson; there one saw violet and lavender and aquamarine and turquoise and lapis lazuli. He had no words for all the colors and shades and tints, had not known that yellow and green possessed such infinite variety, that purple was not merely one purple but a hundred different purples, each one rich and luminous.

For hours and hours, thought of food and drink forgotten, Ran and Norna wandered on through the incredible luminescent forest of the Plain of Lights. This, then, was the "city" which Wild tradition had ascribed to the rorks—a guess no wilder or more erroneous than his own. She needed no explanation, a wonder was a wonder. But his own mind groped and sought, in the end coming up with nothing better than recollections of luminiferous bacteria found on the skin of certain sea creatures; and the cold, cold light of phosphorescent wood and water.

For endless ages this glory had been here, and no human eye ever saw it close before. It was worth hunger, thirst, discomfort; flight, cold, pain, and the fear of death. Hand in hand at first, arm in arm, later; at last, embracing, side by side, they walked on into Eden. It had been inevitable that, sooner or later, sometime on this flight together, flesh should join with flesh in the holy act of love. But they had been preoccupied with other things—simple survival—and their bodies had been taut with fright and cold. Presently, still dazed with visible joy, their faces turned to one another, and they kissed, and then kissed again. He spread the two pelts upon the ground. Some mild warmth seemed to emanate from the brilliant, light-giving plants as he uncovered her breasts and kissed them; and then, her arms around and her hands upon his back, he sank down upon and into her. And all the morning stars shouted together for joy.

For Norna the past had now ceased to exist and the future had yet to take shape. She was Ranny's woman, now. It was all very natural and uncomplicated for her. But Lomar hardly felt that way. The natural exultance inevitable to the male who has been a woman's first male existed side by side and somewhat apart from a growing but not particularly deep affection for her. Then, too, there was the question of what would happen to Norna when they got to the Guild Station. Could he keep her in his own quarters as his mistress? Surely she could not go and live among the shameless and squalid Tame Tocks! What would the Station's attitude be; how would she be treated? For her to return alone to her own country now seemed impossible.

And, not urgently, not constantly, came the last question—and came again—and again: What about Lindel?

They had passed on with great reluctance through and from the Plain of Lights and up onto the more rolling hill country beyond it. The first night away, they could still see the wonders, like a table spread with jewels, from the distance; but after that, no more.

Rorks now began to appear more numerously, nesting in less cover and concealment than before, perhaps because no human feet were known by them to pass this way. The two of them continued to give wide berth to the creatures. Now and then a low, dull grumbling and clicking was heard from the somnolent things, but if they were ever noticed by them, they saw no signs of it. That is, no rork ever seemed to move more or "speak" more because of them. But once again, passing through the frostbitten and sered ranks of redweed, they began to have the feeling that they were being watched.

By Lomar's calculations, inexact as they must be, he and Norna were just about at dead center in Rorkland. The next landmark, assuming that they passed near enough to see it, would be Hollow Rock; after that they could sooner or later expect to see Last Ridge up ahead of them. The storms and other bad weather that had beset them at the start were now seen no more, and a series of several days of calm, dry cold succeeded one another; the entire arc of the ascent and descent of Pia Sol clearly visible in a clear and cloudless sky.

In the shelter on Tiggy's Hill, just before leaving it, Ran had noticed something half-buried in the dirt and rubbish of the floor. It was an old pikehead, dull for most of is edge, but sharp enough in one place to make him wonder if it had not been in process of being sharpened when some sudden alert (or slow drunk) had caused it to be dropped and forgotten. He groped and prodded and was rewarded with the find of the whetstone. Both had been popped by him, yawning, into his pockets, and had stayed there. He was not reminded of them until, during a pause for a rest on one crisp morning, he noticed a dead sapling on the ground which seemed just about the right size and weight for a pikestaff.

The work required to fit the wood into the socket was not considerable, and, while Norna, sitting with knees drawn up, looked on and laughed, he lunged and feinted with it as he had seen the Wild Tocks doing. And, in so doing, lost his footing, and tumbled, crying out in mock alarm, sliding down the slope of ground. He was scrambling to his feet with the aid of the staff when he heard her scream.

"Behind you—behind—kill it—*kill it*—!"

The rork was huge, and, somehow, he got the impression that it was very old. It squatted in its nest, leaning a bit to one side. He could see its flanks moving with the slow breath. Something shriveled and dirty clung about in folds, and the surface of its flesh where this tattered something met the body was sore and broken and oozing. The thing was shedding its skin.

With a movement so sudden that he felt his arms almost snap in their sockets, he raised the pike up above his head, holding it with both his hands. In another second he would have brought it down into that alien and fearful flesh before him—but that second never came. His motives were not clear to him—horrified fascination, perhaps, mingled with a measure of compassion for the now helpless creature—he refrained. Norna did not scream again, but he could hear her terrified whimper as the rork slowly, and surely painfully, lurching and scrabbling, turned itself around.

It smelled—pungently, and hideously unfamiliar. It resembled nothing he knew—and the nonresemblance was terrifying. It was not even to be identified with the supposedly harmless rork of the old 3Ds, for the yellow outlines of the mask were crumpled and distorted by the process of the shedding of the skin. The talons now digging into the ground with the weight of the body and the effort of turning were long and sharp and hideous. The noises coming from the thing had the quality of nightmare.

And yet he could not bring himself to plunge down the pike and then run for safety, knowing that safety was certain enough.

His flesh had been rigid while all this was going on. And then it shuddered and twisted and crawled, while the rork, finally "face" to face with him, made the old Tock tale come suddenly—frighteningly—shockingly true.

It spoke to him.

CHAPTER FIVE

The rork's internal apparatus, vocal, thoracic, and otherwise, must of course have been vastly different from the human; or even the mammalian. The sounds rumbled, echoed, clicked, did things for which he had no names. He felt as though he were reliving the dream in which a rork had talked to him, would perhaps in another second awake. The fact that the sounds seemed to settle into words, words which he understood, increased this sensation, driving him into a kind of vertigo in which his very mind was imperiled, for the words were similar to those of the dream.

Then, in a second, everything became real. There was a difference. The dream-rork had said, *I kill*. And the real rork . . . what was it saying?

Not kill.

Not.

Muscles twitching and jerking, but growing calmer, he lowered the pike. Behind and above him he heard Norna's shuddering breath break off, heard her fall. He half-swerved, legs tensed to mount the slope. And realized that the rork's words might not have been addressed to him.

Two men were standing there, clad in what he presently realized were cast-off rorkskins, clubs in their hands. They were men as certainly as he was a man, nothing at all alien in the lineaments of their bodies. It was their faces that were utterly different, and the difference was not physical. Their eyes did not look at him as he knew his eyes to be looking at them. Their mouths were not fixed in the same lines, nor their cheeks, nor their brows. It was nothing that he could have been able to describe, that difference, but it was instantly obvious, and infinitely significant.

He knew that these men had never grown up among other men than themselves.

And he knew now what had been following him.

One of the men, looking at him with an expression which might have been serene—or might have been something so infinitely alien that he, Ran Lomar, had no conception of it—looked at him and said, "Not kill." It was a human voice, but it was a quite strange voice, and there seemed somehow to be something of the rork in it. It meant that Lomar would not kill the rork, that the rork would not kill Lomar and the two new men would not kill each other. It was not a warning, not a plea. It was a statement.

And Lomar believed it.

He put down his pike, head first into the ground. "No . . ." he said, his voice unsure, his mind certain. "We won't kill . . . Let me . . . I must go up to her. . . ." He gestured at Norna, still unconscious. One of them reached out a hand, he took it, was helped up the slope. His knees stopped trembling. He knelt beside her.

"Dirl sick?" the man asked. And he made a commiserating, comforting sound with his lips, such as one makes to a child. To a baby.

To a baby!

Lomar's head snapped with the shock of it. He knew in that moment of realization who these men were and why they were different. He cradled her head in his lap and patted her face. The other man made the same reassuring, regretful sound. "Poor dirl," he said. Behind them, the old rork groaned painfully, grunted, settled down again into its nest. And Norna opened her eyes.

It was at first hard for them all to understand one another. Lomar's vocabulary was a totally human one, and in this respect vastly larger than the two men's. But they could speak the language of the rork, and often did, until they realized that he could not, then ceased. Some of their talk was in human tongue, though infinitely corroded—with effort, he could make it out. But they seemed to have words of their own, not rork-talk, yet unknown to him. *Yulloa*, for example, had something to do with food . . . or eating . . . or hunger. He could not quite understand what, though. And *ung-guoa-din*—or something like that—had to do with the land itself, or traveling over it; but however often they repeated it, gesturing, it never made sense to Lomar.

The taller of the pair—he called himself *Tun*—dimly remembered his own origins. There was a woman and she had had another, smaller child, one at her breast. And there was a man. A fire. He had gotten lost. He

86

cried into the night and the darkness, and the night and the darkness had cried back at him. Terror, fright, wandering, and the thousand wailing voices of the night. And hunger. Then came a something out of the blackness and picked him up and took him away. Fed him, warmed him with its own body. And in the daylight, played with him.

The other man of the two had been born—and with simple, vivid gestures which admitted of no misconception, he described the process of human birth—here in Rorkland, and knew nothing else. His mother? He pointed to the earth itself, calmly, with the slightest of shrugs. His father? His hand gestured, distantly.

Lomar thought of the difference between the fact and the fiction. Here were the "stolen children" of the old Tock legends. The lost infants. In the darkness no human ear could tell the sound of a human child from that of the crybabies. But—*the rorks could tell!* Far from having been eaten, the lost infants had been adopted. Far from having met with cruelty, they had met with kindness. He contrasted their treatment with that accorded the young rork captured by men, and the contrast made him shudder.

From time to time the old rork nearby groaned its pain and its discomfort; and the two rork-men spoke to it soothingly, caressed it where the touch would not be painful. Repulsive, frightful as it was to Lomar, the rork was obviously regarded with the utmost affection by the two other men. Evidently the relationship between them passed beyond mere symbiosis, although just what that relationship might consist of was more than he could guess at. He recalled his mother, on Old Earth, playing with a kitten. . . . No, it afforded little parallel.

If he was bewildered, Norna was terrified. She clung to him, understanding nothing of what he was trying to tell her. There was a rork! A rork! Nearer than she had ever been to a rork before!—nearer than anyone she had ever heard of had been to a rork. . . and lived. She wouldn't look at it, covered her ears rather than have to hear it, trembled, trembled, trembled.

It was no wonder to her that the rork could speak; everyone in Wild Tockland knew that they could talk; it did not make them a bit less frightening. On the contrary.

87

"Leaves us run away," she whispered, over and over. "Oh, leaves us run and hide . . . hide . . . Ranny . . ."

The presence of the two newcomers did nothing to reassure her. They were as naked as not, they touched the rork, spoke the rork's language, wore the rork's cast-off skin. How could one know that they were, in fact, not men at all? not *real* men—perhaps they were really rork! assuming for the moment and for some evil purpose, the form and shape of men. *Were-rork!* She did not know the phrase and only guessed at the concept. Lomar could see another Tock legend growing before his eyes.

Nor were matters made any easier when the smaller of the two (his name, as clearly as Lomar could master it, was *N'kof*) most matter-of-factly propositioned her. Her shuddering refusal, he received as calmly as he had made the offer. One proffered a drink to a guest, the guest declined the offer, it would be impolite as the host to notice the impoliteness—inexplicable as one might find it —of the refusal.

In the end they did go away; that is, Lomar and Norna and Tun did. Lomar had some notion that the departure was intended to relieve the old rork of the discomfort of their presence; but he was not sure. Communication between them was improving, but it was still largely a sometime thing as far as clarity went. N'kof was to remain behind until the process of casting the skin was completed. He and Tun attempted to explain why this should be so, but whether it was to guard the almost-helpless creature from physical harm, or merely to keep it company, or because there was some especial tie between them, either they could not make him know or they did not care to try.

So the three of them headed north, where only two had been bound before. Tun made no comment on Norna's fear of him, but he walked on the other side of Lomar and at some little distance away; nor did he thereafter ever come closer to Norna or speak to her. The pace was slower now; it seemed quite clear to Lomar that the main reason for hurry no longer existed. The weather was even benign, and Tun knew of so many places where food was to be found—here, a cache of edible nuts; there, a hollow tree or a cave with fungus; pond whose frozen waters, pierced, yielded fish—that they were hungry no longer.

88

They walked more slowly, they paused to eat, they paused to admire (or at least examine) views. But most of all they talked. There was much to talk about, but all of it was difficult, yet gradually became less so. And every hour that passed as they paced up snowy hills and strolled along glades lined with frost-browned redwing plants, under huge and ancient trees, Ran Lomar gave thanks in his heart that he had (for whatever reason) not killed the rork as it lay helpless before him. To this and to this alone he probably owed his life and Norna's and the presence and guidance of Tun. For this man was no philosophical pacifist, no nobly savage vegetarian. His club cracked the skull of a rip which had once ventured too near—Norna clinging, shrieking, to the arm in which Ran held his pike—and more than once, skillfully thrown, brought down game.

Counting at first on their common humanity, Ran was a while in realizing that it was not this at all which made Tun not his enemy. In every way the latter regarded himself as closer to the rork than to other, strange men. It was because Lomar had not killed it when he could that Tun was now—if not his friend, then his companion. Ran reflected on the old principle that "a child raised among wolves will be a wolf"—not, of course, physically, but— in a way—mentally. How far did this hold true of Tun and his like? He walked erect and not on all fours. . . . For one thing, Tun was not alone in being fostered by rorks. How many such "adoptions" there were or had ever been, neither he nor Ran Lomar had any idea. Nor did either know how old the oldest such foster child had ever been. But obviously some of them had been old enough to talk.

The small wanderlings, then, did not come altogether as so many *tabulae rasae* among the rork, and their human qualities and attributes and attitudes would have been in some measure maintained by the other humans they found in rorkland. *In some measure* . . . it would take years of close scientific testing and observation to determine even approximately how large that measure was. True, and inevitably, these people had been influenced by the rork among whom they grew up. But, just as a ray of light passing through a translucent substance emerges tinged and colored by that substance, so the influences of the rork must have been transmuted by the vastly different nature of the human material.

It was a new and fascinating subject for research, but for now it must be confined to speculation. And speculation considered the matter that Ran had encountered none of these people in South Rorkland and had never heard of any in North Rorkland. He mentioned it to Tun, who mentally translated the reply into customary language.

"We stay in the heartland. We are afraid to be seen by the other men. If they kill our big ones they might kill us, too."

Far from loathing the briar patch into which they had, so to speak, been thrown, they actually sought the safety of its deepest part. Far from the rorks being monsters and ravening man-eaters, the rorks were basically peaceful. But—Ran had to ask—did the rork never attack men? Were *none* of the stories true?

"Can you fly, Ran'*k*?" Tun asked, adding a rork-like click to his name as he always did when addressing him.

"No . . . of course not."

Tun rumbled thoughtfully, seeking words. "No . . . you cannot fly. So, the big ones cannot attack you if you do not attack them. They cannot. They do not want to. They *can*not. But if you attack them, they can. They do. Why not?" Why not indeed? Apparently, then, the rork were nonagressive by instinct.

From time to time as they progressed along their way, Tun, without a word, would sit down and become incommunicado, giving no sign that he either saw or heard them. Sometimes he was silent and sometimes he would rumble very softly, wordlessly, for all that Ran could tell; and always, at such times, he faced the sun. He was unable later, or unwilling, to explain this; merely shrugging slightly, smiling faintly his curious, indescribable and quite alien smile.

"Do the rork do this?" Ran asked.

A slight movement of the head, a slight movement of the hand, the little shrug, the mystic smile.

The rork . . . For centuries, men on Pia 2 had believed that the rorks were sharks. Now Ran was learning that they were actually much more like porpoises. There was much, much, much to learn.

90

Another man of the foundling sort, he was, thin and red-haired, red-bearded; and he had come down from a hill to speak to them. Tun had said nothing, nor Lomar, nor Norna—she hadn't even moved or made a gesture. But, as if sensing her fear, the man approached circuitously, avoiding her by some distance; and then, with unfamiliar sounds and incomprehensible gestures, came up to Tun and only then began to speak.

What he had to say was obviously distressing to him and to Tun. When their talk paused for a moment, Lomar interrupted to ask what was wrong.

"Up there—" Tun gestured. "—a man and three rorks. All shake."

"Shake?" puzzled, Ran repeated the word.

The red-haired newcomer looked at him gravely, threw his head back a bit, said, hesitatingly, "Fee-ber." Then, graphically, illustrated his meaning.

"Fever?" Sudden comprehension. "Tock fever?"

"Tah'*k* fee-ber," agreed the red one. Tun made his familiar, regretful, consoling noise. There was nothing that anyone could do, no one suggested even trying to do anything, and so, with more antic gestures and sounds, they parted.

The country through which they now began to pass was one of broad meadows, with yellowed grass still thrusting forth above the thin snow. Ran reflected how different the history of the continent and those who dwelt upon it would have been, had cattle of any sort been introduced in the first settlement. But the Outside had apparently regarded it from the beginning merely as a source for redwing, and this it had remained. He wondered if the good which the plant had done the rest of the Galaxy made up for the ill it had done and was doing to its native world.

And then, almost with a click, he came back to the most immediate present. So—Tock fever had penetrated here; had perhaps been carried here in the person of some foundling child; and even the rorks were susceptible to it. A disease which afflicted different species was by no means unknown. Still, still, he was assuming, jumping to conclusions. Perhaps the malady had its origin among the rork and had passed from them to the Tocks. What its effects might be upon the rorks, he did not know. What its effects were on the Tocks, he knew full well.

Something else occurred to him, and he asked about it. When the rips swarmed—

"Not through here, not this part of the country," Tun said. "Not this last time. Usually we have warning of when they are coming, which way they are going. And we get out . . . when we can." As for the rorks "leading" the rips: never. Those which Ran and Harb had seen racing in advance of the swarm had been fleeing before them. Usually the big ones could amply hold their own against the smaller predatory creatures. It was only during the cyclical periods when the latter swarmed, that they were too many for the rork.

Thus the education of Ran Lomar continued as he and Norna and Tun advanced north. More could have been learned, more seen and experienced, if Norna had not been with them. Although her fears of the strange men seemed to abate considerably, they never entirely vanished. As for the rorks, her attitude changed sufficiently so that she would not run, screaming, at the near sight of one . . . if it were not so near . . . if Lomar was right next to her, if he did not move nearer to it. But more than that she did not change.

Nor did she ever develop any curiosity about them; this irked him the most, but his annoyance ebbed when he realized that the rorks did not seem to have a very great curiosity about them either. Perhaps because Tun was sufficient passport, and, beyond the guaranty of peace that his presence afforded, other questions did not much matter; perhaps because they were still affected by the cold and the changes their bodies were undergoing.

So they passed Hollow Rock, towering in the distance, and one day, walking down a narrow pass between overhanging ledges of rock and hearing the slow drip, drip of the waters, some few days before sighting Last Ridge, Norna herself put it into words.

"Ranny?" she said, pausing and looking at him with a mixture of pleasure and perplexity. "Ranny? Listen. . . . The snow is melting."

"Yes. It usually does at this time of year. . . . Doesn't it?"

Half-annoyed, half-playful, she hit him a light blow at

the shoulder. "Yes, *it* does melts usually. But, Ranny, it means that Cold Time is just abouts over—and we be just about there, to North, to Guild.

"And we be still alive!"

CHAPTER SIX

Tun would go no farther when Last Ridge was sighted. He had told them that he would not, but his vanishing without a word was so unexpected that Ran called and they looked and waited for quite a while before accepting that he had really left them.

There was a smoke on the Ridge. The two of them greeted it with one of their own, and so they did not find that their coming was unexpected. The smoke had not been intended for their benefit. One Shortey, a Tame Tock, had taken a notion to go and fish the series of ponds fed by the same pool in which (it seemed a million years ago) Lomar and Rango had bathed. With him went his current woman and a half-grown boy who was certainly her son, possibly Shortey's son, and possibly her own half-brother. The familial relationships of the Tame Tocks were often complex enough to baffle a combined team of anthropologists and geneticists. The fire had been kindled for nothing more far-sighted than grilling a meal.

The presence of a smoke way up in the middle of the air could not have created more alarm in Shortey's housey than did the one emerging from Rorkland. Probably because of the prevalence of fever, no hunting party had gone thither that Cold Time. What the fire might portend, therefore, Shortey could not guess, and did not intend to try. He took off in the general direction of Tocky Town, followed at a very short distance by the morganatic Mrs. Shortey *de facto*. The boy, nicely calculating the distance of the other smoke against his adolescent appetite, remained behind to wait for the fish to finish.

Last Ridge had sunk into the twilight, emerged again from the dawn, and was gradually growing larger when Lomar's attention was attracted to a drone from overhead. He loped off into a clear spot, dragging Norna with him, and waved wildly to the skimmer with the Station Officer's banneret streaming from the fantail.

"Cute, you have given me one Hell of a winter," said Tan Carlo Harb, his large face grave.

"We haven't had such a pleasant one ourselves," Lomar answered. "Oh—and allow me to introduce Miss Norna . . ." His voice trailed away. For the life of him, he could not remember her family name; she, seemingly stricken dumb, did not help him. "She's the Mister Mallardy's kinswoman, and Old Guns's daughter." Something made him add, "She's my . . . not my *daughter*, damn it, but—"

The SO said, "I quite understand. I *think*. *Well*. You had better hop aboard, don't you think? Before something with eighty-seven legs comes bounding out of the bushes and does simply unspeakable things to us. *Hop!*"

They hopped.

Below and behind them Rorkland receded into a post-impressionistic mist. Seated once again in the skimmer, with its familiar smell of fuel and preservative and the SO's scented waters, the SO's familiar presence and uniform, Ran felt a curious kind of was-it-all-a-dream sensation creep over him. Once again in his ears rang the coarse, loud shouts of Flinders and of Flinders' men, the rumbling of the rorks, the singular intonations of Tun's voice. On one side of him was the clean, well-tailored, well-nourished form of the SO. But on the other was Norna, still in the same dress she'd had on when kidnapped—

"I don't wish to sound offensive in any way at all," Harb said, his face turned away. "But the face of the matter is, you know, that I'm afraid you've been in recent contact with something, well, un-*pleasant*, and, well . . ."

Lomar laughed. "The fact is," he said, "we both stink? Don't we? It would be a miracle if we didn't. Funny, though. On Old Earth I began to miss hot water if I'd been away from it for an hour. And—"

"In the glove compartment," Harb said, stiffly, "you will find an atomizer. Please do not take anything personally. Just *spray*."

Spraying, Ran concluded, "—and this time I never even thought about it. . . . There . . . How's that?" A spicy, somewhat cloying odor settled around them.

Harb turned his head. "Oh, ever so much better. You

94

will notice. That I have not asked you. One single word. About where you have *been*. Let alone *why*. But. If you continue. To say nothing. I. Shall scream. *Well?*"

Ran let his breath out slowly. "Well . . ." he began. Beside him Norna huddled, mute, afraid even to lean over the side or peer through the window.

"Common sense tells me that you cannot possibly have come all the way from the South on foot and with this young person. Not all through Rorkland. Impossible. But logic tells me that you must have. You are such a rather disgusting young hardnose, you know . . . I'm afraid that you did . . . even though you couldn't. *Well?*"

The snowy fields, the smell of slow-burning match punk, the sour, starved stench of Flinders Camp, the sullen gaunt escarpments of the great black Crag, the freezing rain and stinging snow, the marvelous multicolored splendors of the Plain of Lights, the rork that talked, the archaic smiles of the men who lived among them like living legends: the whole unpremeditated fulfilment, and so much more! of his dream plans for his life on Pia 2 . . .

He had not even realized that he had begun to talk until the SO brought the skimmer down, and in the unexpected silence he heard his own voice.

As far as any effect was concerned, he might as well have held his breath to cool his porridge. It would be too much to say that Tan Carlo Harb did not believe him, the man obviously did believe something of what he'd been told, but how much was questionable. The summing-up went about like this.

Lomar's long absence: "Obviously not your fault."

Murder of Old Guns: "Too bad; should have known better."

Kidnapping of Ran and Norna: "Rough notions of hospitality they have down there, eh, cute?"

Flinders' scheme to attack Guild Station: "Ha ha ha ha ha!"

The Plain of Lights: "Quite a sight, eh?"

Rorks can speak: "So can parrots, you know—'Polly wants a redweed,' eh? Hee hee!"

The foundling-men: "Fattening them for the kill. Tsk."

And so it went, and so it went, until, finally, "Well, well, well, too bad. A whole winter shot to Hell. Worry?

You have no idea how I worried about you. Now. What I want you to do. Take your nice hot shower . . . and don't spare the soap. Get a good night's, mmm, sleep—" Sly side glance at Norna, "—and in the morning get yourself down to the Medical Aide. You've had a bad spell of, well, something or other, and we want to make *sure,* don't we, that there are no weeny bugs lingering on in your system. And then come to dinner. I've unpacked a new game I'm eager to play with someone of reasonable intelligence. Trot, now."

No orders to call out the troops, no instructions, no questions, no plans, and barely any interest.

"I might have known," he said to Norna. But it was just one incident among so many, and there was so much else to do and to think about. *A hot shower . . .* It was the first one that Norna had ever had which wasn't a bucket and wash-rag affair, and Ran's own eagerness in his own lustrations didn't prevent him from teaching her how it was done. The shower lasted for several hours, with interesting sidelights and more than one new game which would have interested the SO, if only negatively.

No committee of indignant matrons called to protest Norna's presence. Some ignored it, others found it a novelty justifying the irregularity, and many were too frozen by surprise to decide on any policy. Washed and groomed and dressed in hastily begged and borrowed clothes, invariably a trifle too big in some places and a trifle too small in others, Norna made a good appearance. When someone's wife and someone's daughter decided that she was safe enough to make friends with, her naive reactions to so much that they took for granted, and even were bored by, amused and enchanted them. She, in turn, was delighted to have for the first time in her life friends of her own sex who were part of a world previously glimpsed only via her father, and later, Lomar.

Norna, then, was no problem. Neither, it turned out, was the Medical Aide, a little grey mole of a man who botanized a bit and played the sarn a bit off-key, and drank more than a bit.

"Nothing wrong with you," the MA said. "Just a bit under the norm for weight. Eat hearty. Care for a drink?"

"I haven't had a drink for—how long? Yes. Certainly. By all means."

Bottles and glasses were deftly and quickly produced from the medical cabinet and the tiny physician happily prepared two noggins. "Dead rorks," he said.

"Cheers," said Lomar, after a moment.

"What do you know about Tock fever?" he asked, after another moment.

The Medical Aide blinked. "Not very much. I don't treat Tocks, you know. I'd need a well-staffed, well-stocked hospital to do that. Oh, once in a while I take care of a servant, glad to do another Guildsman a favor. Otherwise I'd be overrun, well, no, have another drink, I'll have one with you, keep you company, no, actually, I wouldn't be. Most of the real bush Tocks, you know, they're scared to death of me, huh huh, can't think why—

"So . . . Tock fever? Oh, it's a sort of low-grade fever that stays on and on. Hard to shake off. Some die of it, some don't. Why?"

The faint, foetal form of a notion was beginning its first stirrings in Lomar's mind. "Do you have any records of the various outbreaks?" he asked.

Mildly puzzled, the little man stroked his lower lip. "No records," he said. "Nooo. . . . That is. Well. What I mean to say—are you interested in botany? Oh. Pardon. I get carried away, hardly an-y-one is interested in botany, besides me. Ah, now, records. I keep a diary. Kept a diary, young man, for for-ty *years*. Whatdoyouthinkofthat?"

Marvelous. Ran thought it was marvelous. In fact, wonderful. The mousy little medico beamed. And in his diary he noted down, as a matter of course, the day's events and the day's reports. Including, when it occurred, outbreaks of Tock fever. It was all down in his diary, a volume per year. Could he go through them and make a sort of chart of the outbreaks, year, month, day? Why? Yes . . . yes. . . . Yes, he could. And in fact, would.

"Take a little *time,* though," he warned cheerfully. "After all, you know, huh huh, for-ty *years*— But I don't mind. Glad to do a Guildsman a favor.

"Are you interested in botany? Oh, I asked— Have another drink."

Ran descended on, rather than reported to, his work with an accumulation of energy that demanded not just relief but satisfaction. He found that during his absence his plans had been allowed to collapse entirely. Business was slower than ever. Old Cap still superintended th slow process of the redwing on its way through the dryin shed, just as he always had, according to the book. Th storekeeper took what the Tocks brought in, making th usual deductions for winter-nipped weed, and handed ou the usual chits. The Tocks bought their clothes, thei booze-makings, new hack blades, and so on, and wen back to their feculent houseys for their usual hanky panky.

And production had continued to go down, dowr derry-down-dee.

He pored over the records, he haunted the curin sheds, he spoke to the Tocks coming in with their bundle of weed; he brooded over his memory of all Rorkland ablaze with redwing, so it had seemed. And when don with this, he sat for hours at his desk, drawing up schemes . . . and then discarding them.

"Have a drink?" said Reldon.

"Have a drink?" said Arlan.

"Have a drink?" said Harb.

"Have a drink?" said Cap.

And Ran answered, "Why . . . yes. . . . Thanks. will . . ."

At nights there was Norna, like a little girl eager t tell of the day's novelties; all, to her, great events. A first this was cute, then it grew dull, then tedious, and finally, annoying. She ceased to bother him, let him tum ble her, fall off to sleep.

One day that grizzled Tom Thumb, the Medical Aide came trotting into his office, crying, "I've never showe you my mosses, have I? Look! Look! See how they'r mounted! All my own system, you know. Now, here w have— Oh, no; no we don't, either. Ah—here—"

Memory stirred in Lomar's mind, first dim, then glow ing.

"Did you ever get around to checking your diary fo me?"

Up from his mosses the little man looked, surprise "Why, yes. Didn't I ever give it you? Oh, I am sorry." H rummaged in his pockets, triumphed. "Here we are. Now yes, the mosses—"

In his hands, the MA, mosses and all, finally gone Lomar had what might be one of the most importar pieces of documentation in the history of Pia 2. On th other hand, failing corroboration, it might be just an interesting piece of paper. He put it away, carefully, and went down to seek the corroboration.

The sunken building that held the massive generators seemed at first deserted, but after Ran had called and shouted a bit, a door slid open and the clean-up Tock appeared. He peered, pulled his head back in, finally reappeared, beckoning. Ran followed him down the shallow ramp and up the corridor, an odd and rather a strong scent growing odder and stronger, ending up in a room bare except for a table, chair, one jug, and some unfamiliar-looking equipment.

Elzel Eads, the Engineering Aide, looked up, wiping his brick-colored face. "Ho, an unexpected pleasure," he said. "You are scientifically inclined, I presume. You should be interested in this little experiment."

"Is that what smells?"

" 'Smells'? Smells, Hell. It stinks. We haven't got all the what you might call bugs ironed out yet." He held up the jug. "Know what this is?" Ran shook his head. A proud smile curved the EA's moon-shaped face. "This is, well, what you might call the triumph of art over nature. Ever heard of tockyrot? Course you have. Turble stuff, isn't it? Just full of *im*-pure-ities. No wonder those poor bastards, so to speak, are all the time sick and stuff. Right, Clud?"

The Tock nodded, solemnly, his eyes on the jug.

"Well, my heart bleeds for those poor sick bastards, so what I have done, I have taken and made a big batch of that stuff—tockyrot, I'm referring to—which is a fermented drink . . . you understand the process of fermentation, as it's called? Right. And I have—get this now—I have *dis-tilled*. Yessir. Distilled all those turble impurities right out of it. And the result, it is as pure and mellow as mother's milk, if you'll pardon the expression. Here. Taste."

Ran tasted, handed back the jug with eyes as moist as his mouth. "That's quite a drink you've made there, Chief," he said, "Thanks. The Tocks ought be grateful." The EA beamed. Ran pointed, paused, swallowed. "That's not a generator, is it?"

Loud was the laughter of the Engineering Aide, that anyone should mistake a homemade still for a generator.

Patting Ran on the back, he led him by the elbow dow another ramp. "*That*—that is a generator. The othe one's on the other side. Quite a difference, hey?"

A hum, barely audible, filled the air. Compared to th generators he had briefly seen in operation on Transfe Ten, this one, Ran reflected, was like a coney to cachalot. But he was careful to appear properly im pressed. "You keep them in beautiful shape," he said truthfully enough. "How high can you get?"

The EA pursed his heavy lips. "Pret-ty high, if th need be. We can get up to 90,000."

"*That* high?"

Eads nodded, ponderously.

"But you don't get them up to that very often, d you?"

"Oh no. No necessity for it. Just when the force field are on. And you know how often that is."

But, Ran pointed out, he did *not* know how often tha was. A discussion followed, proof was—in the mos friendly fashion—sought for; and—in equally friendl fashion, though after considerable searching and fum bling, provided. During the process, the jug was applie to as often as the files. Ran left the engineering buildin somewhat at an angle He thought it best to pause a whil for the present.

Norna was in the room when he came up and starte peeling for a shower. "Hello," he said. "So early? What' with your new friends?"

She mumbled something. He continued to strip. Afte a moment he said, "What?"

"They're tired of me, says. Why not? Just a Wild girl doesn't know anything . . ." Her voice died away in mumble again. For a moment he hesitated, naked, in th doorway. An urge to sit beside her, comfort her, go some where or do something with her, began to rise. But hi head was still muzzy, he needed the shower; then h wanted very much to get onto the next step in his re search. So he said nothing, went in, and let the water play on him. She was gone when he came out to dr and dress.

An ancient astronomer, so the primerscans had re ported in his childhood, ad almost nauseam, once cal culated where an unknown planet must—if it did indee xist—appear and be seen by telescope. Every eye possessing the instrument was presumably pressed to it at the moment prophesied, when, lo, the new planet swam as scheduled into ken. Although Lomar had often enough been bored into wishing the ancient never born, he now consciously reveled in the same joy.

The so-called baby computer, which was the only one Guild Station ever had, had been outmoded when it was first shipped there; but it was good enough for Ran Lomar's present purposes. He provided it with two sets of data, he received one graph. What he had first (he scarcely knew why or how) suspected was now confirmed. The science of epidemiology would demand, and rightly so, further evidence: microbiology, control groups, so on. The science of microbiology was not represented on Pia 2. The evidence was enough for Ran Lomar.

GM : Month II, 3rd Day— Month II, 13th Day, Year 600 (New Cycle)
TF :   Month III, 2nd Day   600
GM : Month IV, 20th Day– Month V, 1st   Day Year 604
TF :   Month V, 22nd Day   604
GM : Month III, 8th Day–Month III, 18th Day Year 611
TF :   Month IV, 7th Day   611
GM : Month V, 17th Day—Month V, 27th Day Year 617
TM :   Month VI, 15th Day   617

And so on, down to this very year itself. The Station's generators were at maximum an average of ten days. An average of twenty days later, there would be an outbreak of Tock fever. The records of the Medical Aide did not indicate how long the outbreak lasted. The fever was considered to be endemic, after a fashion; it never entirely died out . . . presumably. No one knew for sure, no one had bothered to check. Guildsmen and their families had all received general immunization as a matter of course. It did not keep them from getting every contagious disease known in the Galaxy, but it was obvious that Tock fever was within the spectrum. Guildmen did not get it. That was enough for Guildsmen.

There was no reason to assume that the Tocks, Tame and Wild, would not respond to general immunization. But the IM, the immunity agent, was prepared a wilderness of light years away, on the other side of the Galaxy; was costly, it was precious. With population control, the Medical Service knew just how much IM it had to

make—it made that much, and no more. There wasn'
any reason to favor the Tocks over the Chickers, th
Two Tribes, Redhaired People, or Poor Greens, or an
of the other have-not nations which did not receive th
benefits of Medical Service. No reason which would pre
vail, that is, in the present stasis-oriented society. If
pressure group of sufficient strength were to be organize
now, pointing out not such bootless considerations a
"humanity" or "mercy," but the utility of healthy Tock
in increasing redwing production; if such a pressure grou
were to labor year after year, decade after unceasin
decade, perhaps in a few generations it might prevail.

And by that time the Tocks might all be dead.

No . . . the MA, immersed in his mosses, mushrooms
and other items of his botanical hobby, had not bothere
to put down the duration of any outbreak of the disease
But it was perfectly clear that each outbreak occurre
approximately twenty days after the generators ha
ceased to be on maximum.

The generators were on maximum only in order to pu
up and keep up the force fields.

And the force fields were put up only to keep out th
rips when the rips swarmed.

Therefore, it was neither that men spread the diseas
among the rorks nor that the rorks contracted it from
men, it was obvious that *Tock fever was spread by th
rips!*

Lomar got up from the chair in which he had bee
examining the chart, and walked away from the com
puter, trembling with eagerness and with ideas. He no
posessed a mere skeleton of knowledge, so to speak
about the source of the plague which was ruining th
Tocks and decimating the rorks—but more informatio
would probably be of little use to him. He was no bette
than the means available to him. Dimly, he remembere
stories about ancient plagues, mosquito-borne, on Ol
Earth. The mosquitoes bred in marshy ground, stagnar
pools, and when these were dried out or covered wit
oil so that the larvae died (could that have been th
origin of the old proverb about "spreading oil on trouble
waters"?), the plague had vanished. Doubtless there ha
been more to it than that. Probably serums and othe
prophylactic medicines had been developed.

But surely this must be basic: *Destroy the main source and the disease will diminish.*

The rips, then, had to be destroyed. And this was the year to do it, after the all but inexplicable swarming was over, when most of them had died and the survivors were not only fewer but—as he had himself observed—sicker and weaker. But most of them were in Rorkland, where men dared not go. How could the thing be done?—if it were to be done at all? Yes, done it must be. And for all his thinking on the matter, he could come up with no other solution than this:

The rorks had as much to gain from the extirpation of the disease as men had; therefore men and rorks ought to work together on the task . . . therefore, men and rorks *must* work together on it. And it was up to him. No one else could do it. But how even *he* could do it, this was what he could not see. *He* knew that the rorks were basically peaceful, yet how could he convince others? The very name was a synonym for fear, for hatred, loathing, cruelty. Why, what was it that the Guildsmen said to each other even in their moments of greatest relaxation? *Dead rorks!*

No . . . such a coöperation was inconceivable . . . except to him.

He should have liked at least to have talked about it with Norna, but one afternoon, coming up for air, determined to make an effort to wrench himself away from his preoccupation and go somewhere with her, he looked for her and found that she was gone.

"Well, you know," said somebody's wife, "*I* liked her and I tried to make her feel comfortable, but, well, not many did. You know how things are here. Stuffy. Fossilized. And some of the others . . . *most* of the others, I guess . . . oh, they are just so scornful and petty, it makes me furious. After all, it isn't as though her mother were a *tame* Tock!"

After all. . . . He could see it plainly enough. And couldn't discount his own blame in the matter, his recent indifference, preoccupation with his work, taking her for granted . . . using her as a mere commodity. . . . Ran Lomar was not much used to self-criticism, it was not a characteristic of his age and society. But he could not escape it now. That is, not altogether. But neither could he keep it up for long.

Said the old Cap, after telling him that batch 490 had been removed from the curing sheds and was ready to bale and that every other batch had accordingly been moved along one shed; the old Cap said, "Well, and I'm not surprised, yes. Blood will tell. Her father I knew him well, Old Guns, but her mother was a Tocky gal and when you come right down to it why what is she herself, yes, but a Tocky gal? Good morning, yes! So it's natural she goes native, off to Tockytown. Wild, Tame, North, South, what's the difference?"

Ran was minded to follow her, apologize, reason, argue, try to bring her back. But the road to Tockytown led past his quarters and he stopped to change his clothes and get rid of the thick and bitter odor of the curing shed. Someone was in his room, someone humming.

"You're back!" he called out. "I'm glad!"

"I'm glad, too," she said. "And glad that you're glad."

"Lindel," he said.

She was sitting cross-legged on his bed, face in hands. She nodded. "Yes . . . Lindel. Did you know I'd be back? I thought that you'd get tired of her. I had a Tocky boy for a lover once. He was always ready, willing, and able. Not to say, eager. But there was nothing else. How could there be?" So . . . well, I did mind, of course. How can I say that I didn't mind? But I waited, and I'm glad. Are you? Are you really? Are you really glad?"

He sat down beside her and lifted his arm and she fitted under it against him so very neatly. He told her that he was really very glad and then, presently, he showed her how much. It was very pleasant having her back, the temptation to let everything slide was strong, and so he yielded, and so the long slow days went on, unvexed.

Until the coming of the Wild Tocks.

The SO had sent for him, and was standing with set face, on the platform of the Reception Hall, commonly called the Powwow Room. Ran had been there only once before, and though he had little liking for ceremonious settings, was mildly impressed by the faded gold decor and the murals done by a long-forgotten artist. The Wild men, milling around uneasily, stopped talking for a moment at Ran's entrance; then began again, but in a lower key.

Ran, at a glance, recognized Jun Mallardy and beak-nosed old Hannit; but then the SO was talking to him in a low voice.

"I should have paid more attention to what you told me, it seems," said Harb. "But I'll apologize another time. These—" he inclined his head towards the Wild Tocks "—have been jabbering and muttering ever since their boats beached this morning, so I have an idea by now what it's all about. Now let's get it done officially and, I hope, completely."

There was no hint of the old queen in his manner now, and, not for the first time, Ran marveled how his superior could turn himself inside out and then back again . . . of course he was never quite sure which was inside and which was outside . . . but this was no time for speculation. Harb's right foot moved slightly over the surface of the pale green carpeting, came down, lightly but firmly. Somewhere the sound of a gong rang out. The moving and mumbling ceased.

"I won't play word games with you," Harb said. "You haven't all come here just to buy hack blades or sulphur. You want to talk to me. I'm here, and I'm listening."

Jun Mallardy cleared his throat loudly and spat on the rug. The act was not contemptuous or defiant, he had wanted to spit and nothing in his habits or background told him not to. He lifted his long, thin face, thrust out his sparse and wiry black beard.

"Old Man's dead," he said succinctly, "and I'm Mister now—"

Owelly interupted him. "The Mister you be's in Mallardy's Country, but Dominis be's the olderst here."

His words were met with grunts of approval. Jun scowled, but kept silent. Old Dominis combed his great white mane, nodded and nodded. After a moment he said, bluntly, "My ass be's too old and thin for such a long seagoing as this. Only for it's maybe's our doom otherwise, I's stayed at home by my firestone in Dominis' Camp, hears. Guildsmen!" His voice, surprisingly deep, rose now in a great cry.

"Guildsmen! We's aksed you and aksed you for more guns, more guns-makings, and it's always 'No' ye says! Be's right?"

105

His fellows growled and nodded. Harb's face did not change. "But now it's no more time for 'No,' hears. Sell us what we needs, says, or we got's to come for takes it—"

Harb said, "Why?"

All began talking and shouting at once. Old Dominis bellowed, received silence. He pulled his white beard, looked up at them with squinting eyes. " 'Why?' Here's why. Flinders wants to comes and raids here. Flinders wants to comes and takes it all, all that be's here—eats, clothes, metal, sulphur, women—*ahhh* . . ." He gestured his inability to sum up all the contents of the mooted plunder, gave a great, resonant sigh. "Flinders says, 'Joins me, and we splits it all. Plenty's for all, be's,' Flinders says . . .

"Now, hears, Guildsmen. We loves ye not. We gots no cause to. But, sure as Pi' Sol shines, we loves Flinders less. We wantsn't to raid with him. We trustsn't him, no, not the length o' his foreskin. Can we takes what ye's got, if we raids? May's be. Can we get blowns to bloody Hell? May's be. We wins, says—then? Ah, then, Flinders be's chief Mister of us all. That be's bad, hears. *Ohhhh*—" again the deep note, resounding in his chest.

He cried aloud their distrust, their scorn of Flinders. It was plain that he and all those with him would rather, infinitely rather, not ally themselves with him for any cause; certainly not for the chancey cause of raiding the Guild Station. But, he continued, in a more subdued tone, but they might have to. Flinders plotted and Flinders planned. Flinders whispered, Flinders was persuasive. Should he, when he thought his time was ripe, decide to strike a blow, many of the clans might willingly go with him.

And then the others would have no choice.

Let not the Guildsmen think, old Dominis warned, to come into Wild Tockland and punish Flinders themselves. No clan would tolerate that interference. No. . . . Flinders was a Wild one and it was the other Wild Ones who would see to him. But they could only do this if the Guild Station would put them, the contra-Flinders people, in a position of armamental superiority over the pro-Flinders clans. The uncommitted would remain at least uncommitted.

If not . . . if Flinders was not put down, and soon,

there would remain no uncommitted clans—and the opposing clans would no longer stand firm: all, all would be obliged to throw in their lot with the hostiles.

"It be's your choice," concluded the Mister Dominis.

Then the others had their say, and they said the same thing. During all this, Tan Carlo Harb had not moved. When the last man had spoken and there was a silence, then spoke Harb.

"Have you done your trading yet?"

Old Dominis shook his snowy head. "No, we's not. We wants to hears, does we gets what we wants? And how much gots we to pays?"

Harb nodded, curtly. "Do your trading. If I give you metal and sulfur—I say *if*—" He interrupted an excited babble of talk, "if I do, it will cost you nothing. It would be worth it to us." Then he let the talk have its out. Heads were shaken, heads were nodded, heads were brought together and talk muttred.

Finally, the old man had one more question. "When tells ye?"

"Tomorrow," said Harb. And walked out without further word or glance. Ran followed him.

To Ran, when they were alone, Harb said, "Here it is, briefly. Of course there is no chance of their breaching our defenses. Or of starving us out. But they might just wipe up and wipe out our own Tocks, the Tame Tocks, for fun or in frustration. And in that case, we would have to retaliate. The result might be that no Tocks would be left, Wild or Tame, to speak of. I shouldn't like that, myself. And—I can assure you—the Directorate would like it even less.

"*Depopulation.* That's not a nice word. My career, such as it is, would be over, thump, done, thump, finished. Such as it is, it's the only one I've got, and I've got other plans for its conclusion than retirement on quarter-pay. Can you imagine me—*me*?—a beachcomber? Why, not to satisfy the mad greed of any savage chieftain. Flinders. That's the one who wanted to hold you for ransom, correct? Yes. I've heard of him. On the face of it, Flinders must go. But. Oh, my aching lights and liver, but. Who knows what the consequences of arming more of these barbarians might be. Who? You. You've lived among them. Well?"

And Ran said, "Well, indeed. This might be just the opportunity I've been looking for. We have until tomorrow, haven't we? I believe that I have rain checks on several drinks at The Residence. Let's go and turn them in. And talk. And talk and talk."

Harb looked at him. Hard. He said, "Very good. We'll do that. But don't forget who I am, boy. In one classical phrase—*We are not amused*."

They had the drinks and they talked; they talked on, drinks forgotten. And finally, eyes rimmed red from lack of sleep, Harb said, "All right . . . All right . . . I'll authorize it. You've persuaded *me*. Now let's see you persuade the Tocks. If they go for it, if it does nothing else, it should certainly take their minds off feuding and raiding. And after you persuade the *Tocks*, let's see you persuade— We'll see. I laughed at you once. I'm not at all in a laughing mood now."

Neither were the Wild ones. They had done their trading and now they wanted to hear the decision. Gaunt, grim, weather beaten, violent of expression, they seemed wildly out of place amidst the elegant little niceties of the Powwow Room; and, not only were they not impressed by them, they were not even aware of them.

Once again Harb toed the button under the carpet, once again the sound of the gong, again the sullen silence fell. The eyes looking up at Harb from under shaggy brows and ill-cut hair were like wolves' eyes, but the wolves were not eyeing a lamb, they were eyeing some creature at least as strong as themselves. Not one that they loved, for wolves love only wolves (and that not often); but one whose powers they, however grudgingly, respected.

Harb said, in the same flat tones he had used yesterday, "I am giving orders for the issue to you of soft scrap metal and sulphur—"

One word arose from the assembled clan leaders and delegates, spoken as one by many throats.

"*Guns*. . ."

It was not a shout; in its soft and gloating intensity it was more frightening than any shout. And their eyes gleamed.

Harb did not even seem to be waiting. If he had paused, his manner seemed to say, it was because he wished to pause. And now he wished to speak. Almost

ike children caught in error, the Wild men avoided his
eye.

"But I want something for it. More than taking care
of the Mister Flinders. Oh, he is to be taken care of.
First things first. But after that I want something else.
This man you know," Ran stepped forward, "he lived
among you last season. Listen to him."

Obviously, they had no wish to listen to him. Obviously
they wished only to take their gun-makings and be off.
But they did listen. They listened without interruption.
Guildsmen would have laughed, but these Wild men did
not. Almost, Ran wished that they would . . . laugh or
protest or something besides standing there and just looking at him, their eyes like pools of night.

He talked to them about the fever. He hadn't realized
that he knew so much about it. How it came on suddenly,
seemingly out of nowhere. A man might be sitting beside
his firestone feeling well as ever, then start to get to his
feet and be unable to rise without help. The inner fire
that wasted, the chills that followed, the trembling of
the limbs, the long weeks of enforced inactivity, and sometimes longer, and, sometimes, death. . . . The crops that
rotted for lack of tending and gathering, the fishing
craft lying idle for lack of crews, the famine which then
lay great upon the land.

"You complain that we don't give you medicine. And
your complaint is not unjust. But, just or unjust, we still
can't give you medicine. It has to be made too far away
and there isn't enough and there never will be. But I
can tell you how to wipe out the fever. And if there is no
fever, there is no need for medicine."

They stood silently, but at least not impatiently. Someone said, "Tells."

Ran took a deeper breath. "You know how Flinders'
men killed Old Guns and captured his daughter and me.
You know that we escaped. Maybe you don't know how
we got here, back to the North, to Guild Station. Shall
I tell you? We came through Rorkland. All the way."

He had them, now; had their undivided attention. He
told them he had talked with the rorks, and he was believed. He told them that the rorks had men living among
them, and he was believed. That both these men and the
rorks themselves suffered from the so-called Tock fever.
And he was believed. Had he told them that the rorks

109

could fly or that they guarded great treasures of gold and jewels, he would have been believed, for he was touching on the deep spring of legend, as much truth to them as the bleak facts of their grim, bleak lives.

Next he spoke about his suspicions concerning the source of the fever, and how it invariably followed the swarming of the rip who contaminated the land. "Kill off the rips," he said, "and we kill off the fever. That's it." Slowly, slowly, they nodded; but their eyes never left him, and in their eyes and on their faces was an unspoken question.

"You want to know *how*? I can tell you this: We can not do it alone. The rorks have always been our enemies but sometimes it is possible to work awhile with an enemy, against an even greater enemy. Aren't you working with us against Flinders? Isn't the fever a greater enemy to you than the rorks are? You can *see* a rork you can shoot it or kill it with a pike. Can you see the fever? Can you hear it rorking? And in the same way, the fever is a greater enemy to the rorks than you are or than we are.

"I don't know for certain if we and the rorks can work together to destroy the rips and destroy the fever that they spread. But we can try. We have to try. Take your gun-makings and make your guns. Take care of Flinders. And then let me try to arrange a powwow with the rorks about this. If they are willing, then you'll have to be willing, too.

"That's our price."

It was Jun who finally broke the troubled silence. "And if we says, 'No'?"

A little, scornful *huh* of breath broke from Lomar's mouth, unsummoned. "Do you know why I'm here?" he demanded. "I'm here for redwing. Do you know why the whole Station is here? It's here for redwing. Do you think—listen—you say that you don't love the Guild. Well enough. And now ask yourselves, *Does the Guild love you?* Yes, you bare your teeth and laugh at the notion! It *is* silly, isn't it?

"So sum it up. The Guild needs you only for redwing. But you need the Guild in order to stay alive. If we don't lick the fever and stamp it out, production of redwing will drop to nothing. And when *that* happens, the Guild Station here will be closed down without a qualm.

110

"And you will be left here by yourselves and to yourselves. And you do remember—*don't you?*—exactly what happened the last time this planet was abandoned?"

Had they dared, they would have leaped upon him then and there and torn him to pieces. He saw it in their widened eyes, naked teeth, flaring nostrils; the convulsive movements of their hands and bodies. Oh, yes. They remembered. But they did not dare. And at length, old Dominis spoke. "It's a mad scheme, be's," he said. "But if you risk it, we s'll risks it, too."

CHAPTER SEVEN

That was the crux of it. The Wild Tocks had no confidence that men could work with rorks. The threat of abandonment was potent . . . almost too potent . . . the mere mention of it had roused to life hatred which was never altogether still. But, without even realizing it, Ran had touched upon a greater point than he had hoped for. *If you risks it, we s'll risks it, too.* The Wild ones thought the Guildsmen all soft. If Ran Lomar, who had passed through all Rorkland, as no Wild man had ever done; if he would risk it again, they dared not refuse the risk.

In the testing, their survival meant less to them than did their pride.

So much for now for the Wild ones; Ran's scheme, if it would work at all, would require the Tame Tocks's aid as well. It would require every person possible. Never at any time had the Guild Station dealt with the Tame Tocks as equals; there had not ever been any "advisory council" drawn from among them, or anything like that. But from time to time the whole number of them had been summoned to hear what the Guild Station wished them to hear and to obey. More often than not the instructions thus delivered had been conspicuous failures: You are not to prostitute your women. You are not to hold big drunks. You must bring in more redwing. Clean up around your houseys. Once or twice the exhortation had proved successful: You must bury your dead in deeper graves so that the rips cannot get at

111

them. You are not to put mud on your weed to make i
weigh more before you sell it.

So, now, at the Station Officer's "invitation," the tat
tered horde came sweeping in from all of North Tock
land. The continued presence of their Wild cousins afte
trading was over had not escaped notice; usually th
fierce Southern men departed the instant commerce wa
concluded. The Tame Tocks did not come obediently, no
did they come with intentions of disobedience. They cam
because coming was an occasion. And they were curious
too. Who knew what strange new thing was now to b
demanded of them? The prospect did not dismay or dis
courage them. Whatever it was, certainly they woul
make a stab at it, if only for the novelty.

This conclave, however, was from its beginning dif
ferent from the others. For one thing, there were Wil
Tocks present, in front of the platform erected an
hastily carpeted in the open space set aside for th
gathering. Bold, brave, savage-looking men, with match
locks, some of them. The Northern Tocks eyed the South
ern ones with mixed emotions—admiration, fear, suspi
cion, resentment. And the Southerners, when they eye
them back at all, showed either indifference or contempt
New, too, to the occasion, was Ran Lomar, the "rea
Man from Old Earth." Aside from his impressive origin
the story of his escape from the wicked Old Mister of th
Crag and his passage through Rorkland had made hin
an almost numinous figure.

The salty scent of the white-waved seas was on th
breeze as it had been when Lomar first set foot on thi
almost lost world months (it now seemed years) ago. H
thought of that as he rose to speak after the SO's brie
opening words. He had wanted no more, at that time
than to be left alone to roam around; to remain un
committed. He had not been allowed to be left alone
nor permitted to remain uncommitted. Roamed? Yes, h
had roamed, all right. . . .

Now, gazing at the sea of faces—dirty, often half
toothless, vacant, vapid, unknowing, stupid, unlearne
and perhaps unteachable—he felt his previous certaint
ebb, his excitement turn sour. What could he hope to d
with these people? To say that it was not their faul
that they were as they were was merely to state
gigantic non sequitur. A sudden wave of indifferenc

112

swept over him. He did not care at all. What was it all to him?—Guild, Station, redwing, rorks, rips, Tocks? If the scheme failed, then it failed. The doom of Pia 2 was not his own doom. There were other worlds to remain unconquered by.

Feeling cool and calm and almost careless, he began to speak. Without thinking about it, he reversed the order of his remarks from what it had been when he addressed the Wild men.

"We Guildsmen built this Station here only to get redwing," he said. "We no longer get as much as we want, and each year we get less. Pretty soon, at this rate, we'll get none at all. And when that happens, we shall all go away."

The crowd stirred uneasily. It had felt an intimation of mortality, but no more. "Do you understand? We shall all go away. None of us will be left. None of us will come back. No one else will come back. No store to sell you things. No force fields to defend you from the rips. The Wild ones have guns. You have no guns. We will leave you none. We will leave you nothing. And the Station will fall in on itself, like an old housey in the rains. *We will not be here again. . . .*"

A moan swept through the crowd. "Do you remember what happened the last time the men went away from here? It will happen again. *Be silent!*" The clamor stopped for an instant, then the moan began again.

He himself was silent a moment. Then he told them about the fever, how it was helping to kill them off, making them fewer and weaker, unable to bring in the required redweed; told them how he had learned of the spread of the fever by the rips. And told them, finally, that their salvation rested on two things and two things only.

"One. The rips must be wiped out." He needed not to labor on this point. They were already convinced. Probably they would have been convinced even if the question of the fever had never entered into the matter. Almost, he could read their minds. *The Men have guns, it will be easy.* "It will *not* be easy!" he shouted. They jumped, startled, sank back, abashed and astounded. And so he passed on to the next and last and greatest matter.

The knowledge that they would have to penetrate

113

Rorkland left them speechless. And the fact that they would, in all probability, be working with the rorks left them stunned. He told them that the rorks could speak; they believed him. They could put nothing past rorks. He told them that their lost children had often not died at all, had certainly not been killed by rorks, were— many of them—now living peacefully with rorks—almost, they believed him. He had only to show them. But —to *work* with the rorks? To enter safely, to remain safely, to emerge safely—

While the Wild ones looked on scornfully, or looked away indifferently; while Tan Carlo Harb sat, impassive in his seat; a wave of noise spread over the crowd, and Lomar let it spread. At length one Tock thrust his way forward. Many started to follow him, but Ran gestured them back.

It was his former guide. He hesitated, then pressed on, fumbling at his bosom. "Mist Ran. . . . You know. . . ." The words came babbling forth from him.

He had a charm. He drew it forth, held it up. It was safe for him to enter Rorkland, and enter it he would—there followed many brave words amounting to the fact that wild rorks could not drag him there alone, but if the Wild Tocks and the Guildsmen (armed) would go, *then* —and so forth. But. There were others who had charms. All would go. Heads were nodded vigorously, bosoms were searched, charms produced, those nearby turning to look and nod as if they had never seen such things before. *But—*

What of those who had no charms?

And most did not.

Lomar opened his mouth, intending to assure Rango, to assure them all, that charms were not necessary. Without having said a word of the sort, he closed his mouth and allowed the general tumult to melt, and though rapidly. Such assurance would be useless. Rorks were deadly, rorks were dangerous, rorks were demons. They all *knew* this. Rational argument, appeal to his, Lomar's own contrary experience, producing the foundlings: all all would be useless.

Behind him he heard Harb's voice, low, challenging even—damn him!—amused. "Let's see what you do with *that*, cute. . . ."

What he did with it was this. "Step aside, you Tocks!

114

Make way, there. Don't prevent the ladydoctors from coming forward. Don't you see that they want to talk to us? Let the ladydoctors *through,* I say. *Move!*"

There were several score of these canny hags in practice. Half witch women, half herbalists, peddlers of potions and poisons. What they had been thinking, no one would ever know. But now, at Lomar's words, they raised their heads like so many snakes, peering anxiously around them. What! Ladydoctors were coming forward? Ladydoctors wanted to speak? Oh! And ho! And help me up and let me by! The crowd, looking all around and ready enough to make way, was soon enough given its chance.

There were withered old crones, hobbling on two sticks, and buxom hussies only just beginning to rot a bit along the seams. There were muttering beldames, thoroughly convinced of their own powers, and shrewd-eyed traders out for the main chance and the last chit; some were sad, some were bold, some suspicious, some eager. Whatever they were and however they were, soon enough they were all up in front, pressing close upon the rather uncertain Wild men.

Right up in front. All of them. Just where Lomar wanted them to be.

"Do you want the Men to go away?" he asked, in loud and ringing tones. "Do you want all the Tocks to die of fever?" And, taken utterly unawares, the women began to protest, rolling their eyes and beating their bosoms; but he cut them short. "You don't! Good! You *will* make the charms, then—won't you?"

Yace! Yace! They would, of course they would! And such charms, too, prepotent and powerful—Again he interrupted. "Enough for all . . . *won't* you?" Too late, the sorceresses began to perceive that a trap had been laid for them; perception overtaking mere suspicion. Enough charms for all? Well, this was something else, now. Charms did not grow on stalks like redwing. They required careful preparation, rare ingredients, and—oh, yace! oh, yace!—costly care. . . . He caught up the words, he cried them aloud, he scorned and defied them. Exercising talents for commerce which would have both astounded and delighted his instructors at the Guild Academy, he beat them down and down and down. And when they showed signs of balking, he informed them that the crowd might turn into a mob. The crowd, of

115

course, immediately showed signs of doing so. And the ladydoctors capitulated, en bloc.

As he had known they would.

And now Ran had to determine the final question. Guild Station, Wild Tocks and Tame, all had agreed. Would the *rorks* agree?

Dominis, Mallardy, the other Misters and their crews, had departed, taken to water for their distant homes. With them had gone the makings for guns and gunpowder sufficient—Ran hoped—to put an end to Flinders forever. The ladydoctors and their apprentices toiled be time and overtime at making charms enough for all the able-bodied males in North Tockland. The Guildsmen, mostly, shook their heads, snickered, doubted, and—inevitably—shrugged, turned to their drinks. The conventional toast, however, seemed to lack something of its usual surety.

On this trip to Last Ridge, Ran went by skimmer. "It's a harebrained plan, cute," the SO said, watching him pull his pack out. "Fortunately, *I* make up the official reports, and if these lovable old monsters of yours turn you into a human shish kebob, well, I shall cry my eyes out without letting one tear drop onto the pages. You understand. For pity's sake, boy, be *care*ful!"

Ran grinned. "You're fond of the classics. Do you remember this line? 'It is a far, far better thing I do now, than I have ever done—'?"

The SO said, stiffly, "We are not amused." His large, expressive face worked a bit. Then he was off. Ran waved him into a distant speck, and, when he turned around, Tun was there.

"I seem full of great quotations today," Ran said, in greeting. "How about this one? 'Take me to your leader'." The rorkman surveyed him with his familiar, strange smile. He touched Ran's arm, gently. The cast skin he had worn was gone now, unneeded in the warmer weather, and he was dressed in nothing but loincloth and leggings to protect against the whip grass. Of course he had no leader, the concept was apparently unknown in Rorkland. They walked together, slowly, and Ran talked.

Ran talked. Tun said nothing, or next to nothing. Now and then, as on their previous tour, he stopped and sat

116

and faced the sun. From time to time he made some slight gesture. He walked like a man. But when they came to a stream or pool, he crouched on all fours, like a rork, and lapped the water. He accepted the food Ran offered with grave courtesy. Occasionally he sang a bit of a song that once must have been totally human; its very tonality now rang alien in Lomar's ears.

When they were still a long way from Hollow Rock they could see its curiously convoluted spire; then coming closer but still not close, Ran could see the rorks and their men moving about at its base. There were quite a number of them, and he did not ask how they came to be there. It was not likely he was finding, coincidently, some regular assembly or rendezvous. Had those occasional little gestures of Tun's conveyed some message to someone or something which for any reason did not care to come into view just yet? Had the near-naked man possession of those supranormal powers which human normality, still striving, had yet to achieve?

"Come, Ran'k," said Tun, placing one hand on his shoulder. No introductions were made, no one seemed surprised or particularly pleased or displeased to see him. He was close enough to the rorks now to hear the gizzard stones grinding inside of them, a curious noise which, he felt ought to make him uneasy. He did not know why he felt it should, or why it didn't.

"In the Cold Time," he said, coming to the burden of the matter at once, "I passed through your land in peace. Now I have returned to it in peace, and this is why. I have learned that the shaking fever which attacks men and rorks alike is spread by the animals we call rips. They must be destroyed if we are all to be well again. If it is not done this year, when they are few and weak, it will have to wait more years until after they have swarmed again. My people, North and South, are willing to work with you. I have come to propose a powwow—that is, that in fifty days, we each send fifty of our number to meet at the great hill with two peaks, Tiggy's Hill, in the far South. We will all come there in peace. And in peace, we will talk of this."

And the rorks and the rorks' men said, "We will come there in peace. And in peace we will talk of this."

It was all very simple.

117

Tan Carlo Harb, calmly overriding the obsessed objections of the Motor Aide, Starchy Manton, had decided that they would go South in the Station's single aerospacecraft, rather than by slow skimmer or slower boat. It was to discuss plans for the trip that Ran came to the Residence one evening, close to the appointed fiftieth day. He found him pale and very disturbed.

"Who would have thought it?" he flung the rhetorical question at Lomar. "Who could have predicted it? It's bad, it's bad."

It *was* bad. It was Flinders. The clans hostile to him had made their arms, pikes and matchlocks, prepared their powder, and marched out upon him. Flinders and his hard core allies were obliging enough to meet them en route, and in the battle had suffered a defeat. So far, so good. But Flinders, not intending to remain defeated, had quickly decided on a strategy. His forces would scatter, thus obliging his enemies to scatter as well if they would pursue them. And he and his clan and the clans allied with them would rendezvous—a desperate measure—in the far, far south of Rorkland.

The place he picked was Tiggy's Hill.

He was there, hiding out with his fighting men, concealed upon the crown, when the first contingent of the rork-folk arrived, casually ahead of the set date for the powwow. It would probably have meant no difference to Flinders if he knew, but he did not know and he did not care. He attacked the delegation. It was not a battle but a massacre. Almost none escaped, rorks and rorkmen. And among the fallen was Tun.

"Oh, God!" cried Ran, in agony. "What they must think of me!" Once again his plans had come tumbling down. Not only, not merely, was his personal success destroyed, not only did the future existence of mankind on Pia 2 receive a probably irrevocable setback. Tun was dead, who had—obliged by no claim known to Lomar—helped Lomar and Norna to live. Tun of the curious smile, naked Tun, Tun strong and alien. Tun dead. And with his death, dead, too, seemingly the chance at what might have been the greatest breakthrough in human history between human and nonhuman.

Lindel was in his room, it seemed that she was always in his room now, talking eagerly of his plans and of how well they were sure to be received by the Guild

Directorate, singing to him, soothing him, making love to him. "Where are you going?" she cried, now. "What's wrong? *Ranny!*"

She screamed at him, told him he was mad, perverse, perverted to think, even to think, of going back into Rorkland now, after what had happened. He would be able to think of something else, she begged. Something sane, safe. "Do you think you can get them to listen to you now? Are you going to be some kind of martyr? Do you want to die? What is it—a sacrifice of atonement?"

"If it has to be."

She held onto him, he put her away, she struggled to pursue; he closed the door on her and locked it.

Last Ridge again. He set the skimmer's controls on automatic return, prepared to climb in. A woman's voice. Ranny. Ranny. Lindel again. Got out. Hurry up, get away.

The remembered, twice-reflected-on voice, broke into his preoccupation. It was not Lindel at all, it was Norna. He turned, calling, "Goodbye, Norna," stepped into the skimmer. Then she had her hand on it. A Tock was with her, cleaner than average, melancholy face, long arms. Her lover, probably. "Goodbye, Norna."

She did not remove her hand, turned to the other. "Goodbye, Dukie," she said.

"No, girl," he said, sadly. Pleadingly. Stroked her arms, her breasts, in free Tocky fashion. "No. . . ."

"Norna, you can't come."

"Why not?"

Quickly, briefly, he told where he was bound, and why. She said, "I wents there with you once, risks and all. I'll go again."

"No—"

"Won't they likelier think you peaceful, they sees me, too?"

He had thought they might, and on that, let her come. But they had not, not at all. The skimmer had returned on automatic, and down into Rorkland on foot they went, Ran and Norna. He scarcely recollected how long it had taken to find the first ones, but if her presence made a difference, it made not much difference.

"Liar!"

"Liar!"

The men menaced him with their clubs. The yellow-masked ones rorked at him, growling and clicking and thundering. They would listen to no explanation, they wanted no more of the sight or sound of him. "Come in peace and in peace talk?" Blood and bodies on the slope of Tiggy's Hill. Liar! *Liar!* Another trick, another scheme.

They gave him and Norna until sundown. That long, no longer.

Watchful, silent, they saw the two depart, defeated. The redwing was growing flush throughout the long glades, but Ran had no eyes for it. He saw it without seeing it, between the great russet leaves and his eyes was the face of Tun, blood but emphasizing his enigmatic smile.

He scarcely understood the pad, pad of running feet, or why Norna scrcamed, or where the rip pack had come from so suddenly. They were thin and gaunt and they whined with hunger and excitement and they seemed to come from everywhere. He did stop, for they were in front of him; he did put one arm around Norna, raised the other in impotent defense. But mostly he was numb, helpless, his mouth slack. It scarcely seemed to matter.

Then one rip squealed, the squeal cut off sharply by the thud of a club. And long and supple feet, caricatures of human hands, deadly claws raked and tore. And still he stood there, moving not. There was a pause.

"We haves come in peace," Norna said. Her voice trembled, perhaps in her heart she still feared the rorks and their men as she did the rips. "We haves no weapons, sees. . . ." She said the things that Ran had wanted to say, and she was suffered to say them out. And there was then another pause.

It was the same band, rorks and men, which had ordered them out, angrily refused to listen. They had followed to make sure of their leaving, grimly determined to destroy them if they failed to climb Last Ridge by sundown time. And now they realized that Lomar and Norna really had put their own lives in jeopardy, and had not . . . probably not . . . been laying another trap

"But it was no trap," Ran found his voice again. "I was not us. Let us make another time, and I will promise you defense. We can meet this time at Hollow Rock Will you trust us?"

Long, long were the shadows in the redwing glades And long, long was the silence. Then it was broken.

"We will trust. We will trust you."

CHAPTER EIGHT

Whatever victory Flinders had achieved by the massacre at Tiggy's Hill did him no good. The presence of the unknown men among the rorks, dead at the foot of the Hill, had caused strange rumors to spread throughout South Tockland. *Men among rorks!* It was more than unheard of—it was unbelievable—yet, it had to be believed.

There was no particular reason in logic why this should have resulted in any loss of face by Flinders. And perhaps it was not exactly face which he did lose. But the matter was strange, the matter was fearful, the Wild people shrank from it; and, since Flinders was connected with it, they shrank from Flinders. The expected rendezvous of the clans allied with him never came about. After waiting long in vain, he broke his bivouac on Tiggy's Hill and decamped.

The union thus interrupted was not one easily put together again. The return of the sachems from the North found their people both restless and uneasy. The story brought back was not one quickly or easily assimilated, and both it and the tentative agreement based upon it had to remain for some uncertain time in the realm of talk. One thing, however, was easily understood:

Guild Station had given gun-makings and sulphur for gun-powder, and both were to be used against Flinders. There was no uncertainty about this. Given more guns, the Wild Tocks had no objection to assailing Heaven itself. Flinders' support melted like soft snow in the spring sun; indeed, it scarcely survived the knowledge that declaring against him would bring matchlocks and powder. Soon every smithy rang with the sound of hammers; seasoned timber saved for years against such a chance was brought out to be turned into gunstocks, and charcoal and stinking nitre was fused with sulphur at the primitive powder-mills: ground, moistened, caked, carefully broken, ground again.

Flinders heard, of course. He would have had to have been deaf in ears and insight not to have. And Flinders did not wait. Down from the Crag he came, raging and furious; attacked Nimmai, was driven back; feinted at Owelly, but did not press his chance; and was caught there between the two when Dominis and Mallardy and the others came grimly up against him. His losses were heavy, and he went limping off like a rork on three legs, nothing but an unexpected rain that doused matches and soaked powder saved him from being killed or captured then and there.

He was counted lucky to have regained the ragged and rocky shelter of the Crag once more, where for the moment none cared to risk following, there to brood upon his wrongs and his rights, his ruined hopes, and his ever scanty larder. The plan of attacking the Guild Station had already receded into the mists which distilled and dripped from the black rocks and the black and mossy limbs of the gaunt trees.

So much, for now, for Flinders.

In some ways the great powwow at Hollow Rock resembled the arrival of the Q Ship. The same huge pavilion was erected, similar (if not quite the same) victualing arrangements were made. There was that air of excitement and movement once again. But there, perhaps, the resemblance ceased. Q Day, by definition, came but once every five years; but it *came* every five years, and, however new it seemed, it was not new and had never been since the first time. The meeting here at the foot of towering Hollow Rock, unique in geological formation, was itself unique in social formation. No one knew quite what to expect.

Harb, Lomar, a number of aides (these still in a state of shock, not so much at the prospect of meeting rorks face-to-face as it were, as having to do without drink for the duration of the meeting), and a number of Tame Tocks arrived as scheduled by aerospacecraft. They saw the smoke of the Wild men's cook fires slowly rising up through the soft air—men: they had brought no women. But, then, except for Norna neither had the Station group.

Morning of the day set for powwow found Northerners and Southerners still alone, and, as the day drew on, Ran became so nervous that he began to regret the SO's ban on booze. There was good enough reason for the ban, most of the Station personnel being basically unstable and hence unpredictable. Such had been known to crack and run amok before; besides, Harb did not feel that a rork would appreciate a toast to "dead rorks," whether understanding it or not.

The Wild ones had held off at first from entering the pavilion, either from suspicion or shyness. While Harb was discussing with Ran how to overcome this—"Isn't it a patriarchal tradition, or something, boy, that if you eat a man's victuals, it's bad form to blow his brains out with a blunderbuss?"—and while Ran, half-listening, was scanning the landscape for signs of the rork-folk, Norna had taken matters into her own hands.

"Jun," she said, coming up to the Mister Mallardy, who stood a bit apart from his fellows; "be's vexed with me because I takens another for my man?"

He eyed her straightly for a moment without talking. Then he said, "May be's if I gones into Rorkland wi' you, you's taken me." She said nothing to this, and he went on, "But I wasn't. I gots no right to be's vexed."

"I'm glad. Then come into the tent-house with me, and we's eats a bite together."

The ice, thus broken, never froze again, and Ran gave over his lookout and joined everyone in the pavilion. Gradually and guardedly there began to grow between he and Jun that rather special kind of relationship which exists only between two men who have competed for the same woman, to the loss of one of them. It was much later in the day when a sudden fall in the congregation brought all eyes to the door. It was one of the Station aides, and it was obvious that he had somehow evaded the ban on booze. In a voice which combined amazement, intoxication, dismay, and befuddlement, he announced loudly and clearly, "Oh, my ass and my ankles —the place is full of rorks!"

They had been asked to bring fifty of their number, and to this they had scrupulously adhered: there were twenty-five rorks and twenty-five of their men. And "men" in this case included women. For the first time Ran— and, of course, the others—saw female foundlings. There were not many of them . . . a young woman, a girl of perhaps ten, carrying an even younger child on her hip, and an old, a very old crone. It was she who broke the silence as those in the pavilion streamed outside.

"Smells," she muttered. "They smells . . ." The pa-

vilion's accommodations included a bathing unit and i'
had been liberally used, but every living thing has its own
incessant and distinctive odor. A life in the wilds of Rork
land had sharpened her senses. The next to speak was
Rango. He took a step forward, scanned the faces of
the assembled rorkmen, said, uncertainly, low at first
then higher, "Butty? Butty?"

No one spoke. Helplessly, he repeated, once, "Butty."
It was no longer a question. Then one of the rorkmen
who had not moved a muscle, stepped slowly forward
Rango looked at him. Then they met and embraced
Rango's face working. But the countenance of his long
lost brother showed only the strange, archaic smile.

Lomar, feeling his eyes smart, said, without turning his
head, "You see now, all of you, how human beings do
live among the rorks. Could you want better proof that
rorks and men can work together? Of course the rork
will attack men—if they are attacked themselves. But no
otherwise.

"Rorks. Will you come forward now? One by one
please, and slowly. Rorks? Come?"

Again the silence. The wind spoke, nothing else. Then
slowly, slowly, on his great and high kneed legs, an old
one, more grey than black, came stepping forward. Half
way toward the pavilion he paused. "Ror'k. C'ome," i
said. And, "Ror'k c'ome in peace." Next to him, Ran
heard someone make a noise in his throat. The creature
took another few steps forward, and sank down, folding
its legs. It was only then that the Tame Tocks seemed
to wake up to what was actually happening. As a second
rork came forward they all felt for their charms, started
to squat down and mumble their apotropaic formula. Bu'
none of them finished doing so. Slowly they straightened
up. Some still continued to hold onto their ju-ju bags
But Ran felt that the first step toward the conquest of
fear had been taken.

And in such a situation, it was the first step which
counted.

Rorkland had to be mapped.

So Ran's thought was, standing there on an unnamed
and rain-soaked hill somewhere in the uncharted heart
lands. Aerial surveys had doubtless long ago been made
and were probably somewhere available. But they weren'

available *now*, and would be of limited use in the present circumstances. It was in filling this gap that the rorkmen were found, unexpectedly, to be of especial help.

One of them came scrambling up to him now, rain streaming from his hair and naked breast and shoulders. "What's ahead down there, Tranakh—in that glen full of ferns?" Ran asked him.

The man told him, half in speech and half in gestures, that the glen widened considerably, that it contained a small brook. It was unlikely, he thought, that any rips were there . . . but there might be.

Ran nodded, and, turning his head, spoke into the small mike-piece on his shoulder, Tranakh trotting back to his scouting mission immediately. In a few minutes a small band of men entered the glen. Ran knew, though he could not see, that another one would be approaching from the other end. If there were any rips in the little cove they would not leave it alive The sides were too steep. He brushed his rainy face and started down the hill, taking with him a long pole with a white flag on it. At this signal other white flags moved on, from far right and far left. Like an irregular wave, he knew, the movement would spread east and west the breadth of the narrow continent.

The war against the rips proceeded its slow, but reasonably certain, pace.

The war was an important one, important by the nature of the enemy. But more—much more—important by reason of the nature of the allies. In one month, he had upset the notions and the habits of centuries. Tame Tocks working alongside of Wild ones—not, not yet, literally alongside or side by side, but at least in the same endeavor—and *knowingly* so. Wild Tocks coöperating with Guildsmen! And, of course, most wondrous of all: Man (civilized, barbaric, degenerate), *Man was working with rork!* It was all very revolutionary, but perhaps it had been swept along in part by its very immensity. Only Flinders and Flinders' Clan, still sullen and recalcitrant in their stronghold on the Crag, held aloof from the campaign.

Ran sighed, faintly, recollecting that this great project in mutual aid was to hold good for only one year. It was too bad, too bad, but it appeared that the time was not yet ripe for an attempt to institute a perpetual concord. For a year, at any rate, the two species (including the four classes of men: Wild Tocks, Tame Tocks, Guildsmen and rorkmen) were coöperating to wipe out the two common enemies—the predatory rips and the crippling disease they bore.

A voice spoke now in Ran's ear, from the tiny speaker plug there. "Skimmer Five, reporting to Command."

"How's it going your way, Motor Aide?"

"Just a bit slow . . . don't let them move too fast ahead, east of center. We don't want to break the line."

"All right. What's the holdup there?"

"Quite a big rip pack down on the coast a ways back—part of it broke through and they had to move the line back to make sure none got away. Hey! I got a few of them, myself!"

"Very good, very good, MO! Anything else?"

"Nothing else for now Skimmer Five, closing out."

Whether it was Tan Carlo Harb's potent powers of persuasion or whether the situation had actually impressed itself upon the Motor Aide, or whatever it was—Starchy Manton had actually broken through at least one of his obsessions and allowed that a genuine emergency was at hand. He had put all his skimmers into use, and his ground craft, too (limited though its value was in uncleared, roadless Rorkland); and was participating with eagerness. Perhaps, too, the fading into the distance of the last Q Day, with its mysterious fears that he would be shanghaied aboard, had something to do with his vigorous emergence from his shell.

Similar things had happened with some of the other Guildsmen. It was reported, for example, that Reldon, in charge of a message center moving up the west coast, had not touched a drop since the campaign began! And old "Cap" Conders, leaving his rank-smelling curing sheds for the first time in years, had thrown himself into the work so enthusiastically that the Medical Aide had been obliged to order him to slow down.

At its most basic, the campaign comprised an irregular rectangle which constantly moved in upon its own center from all four sides. The Tame Tocks comprised the Northern Line, moving steadily south. The Wild Tocks, on the other hand, constituted the Southern Line, and moved steadily north. In both cases "steadily" was merely approximate. When these two longitudes reached set points

126

as they worked towards each other, the rorks whom they would find waiting for them would commence moving inland from the coasts; the Western Line moving east, the Eastern Line moving west. As all four lines gradually decreased the area of the rectangle they naturally were spread less thin.

And a good thing, too!

Usually the hunted rips did not wait for the lines to come within striking distance, but fled upon their approach. First came the men, armed with pikes and hacks and clubs and guns. Behind them, the women and boys, drumming on everything that would drum and clashing everything that would clash; meanwhile shouting and howling and making shrill ululations. Where the ground was clear enough for the skimmers that passed continually back and forth aloft to see that no rips lay closely near ahead, the spaces between the people was increased: else they would have driven a good part of the ground fauna of Pia 2 ahead of them; instead the animals were allowed to pass through the gaps in the line.

The speed of each line and of each section of line naturally varied with weather and terrain. On clear days, cool and crisp, over the grassy flats and low rolling terrain, which would have made and might yet make such excellent pasture, the going was good. Rain, excessive heat, gullied and broken ground, all would slow up the passage. Mountains and valleys, naturally, reduced it to a crawl; thick forests, swamps and brambles, heavy stands of whip grass—there were no great rivers in Rorkland, none that could not be forded except when the greater rainy season had increased them to torrents.

The white flags of the command posts sometimes swept along, sometimes picked, sometimes felt their way. Down from the yellowgrass, the sloping hills and salt-scented seacoasts of the North; up from the black-mossed rocks and valleys of the South—through the redwing glades, again aflame with rich color—now wet, now dry—they pressed on. And finally, on the west coast the Wild Tocks made first contact with the waiting rorks, and paused. Shortly afterwards the Southern line reached the Eastern one, too. It took a while longer before the Northern line touched either Eastern or Western Rorks, and began Phase Two of the campaign.

127

Once before, looking down from a skimmer, Ran Loma[r]
had seen a line of rorks and a mass of rips. But the rip[s]
had been in swarm then, uncountable, and the rorks ha[d]
been fleeing. It was different now.

As far as his eye could see the line went on in bot[h]
directions, advancing westward with almost military pre[-]
cision. He could hear the stamping of the feet, see th[e]
haze of dust, feel the vibration of the rorking. The yello[w]
masks bobbed about, the stalked eyes swung all aroun[d.]
Few as the rips were now in comparison with their num[-]
bers the year before when their population had explode[d,]
the growing concentration was resulting in ever-large[r]
packs of them. From time to time such a group woul[d]
form and for a while attempt to hold its ground, teet[h]
bared, bristles high. But the line of rorks never faltere[d;]
invariably, the rips gave way.

Rather late, admittedly, a frightening notion had oc[-]
curred to Lomar. If the rips spread the fever as they ad[-]
vanced, would not those advancing now find the feve[r,]
so to speak, waiting for them? The little Medical Aid[e,]
startled so thoroughly out of his preocupation with mush[-]
rooms that he might never return to them, threw himsel[f]
into this question with agitated enthusiasm. Rips were cap[-]
tured, killed, dissected, organs probed and peered a[t,]
slides and solutions made and examined, soil samples sub[-]
jected to a variety of tests—the very water and the ver[y]
air was trapped and tortured to divulge its evidenc[e.]

Finally, the verdict.

"Mind you, mind you," the small physician urged, cau[-]
tion finally overtaking enthusiasm; "this is a provision[al]
opinion—merely provisional, merely an opinion. It's n[ot]
an official report."

And Harb, sweaty, grimy, impatient: "Either *talk,* boy[,]
and talk *fast,* or—"

So, hastily, not waiting for the sentence to be con[-]
cluded, the MA talked. Traces of latent fever were foun[d.]
Almost no evidence that it was now active among th[e]
rips. And more, and more:

". . . in fact, it's my opinion that, well, naturally, th[e]
same disease affects different organisms differentl[y,]
wouldn't you agree? so it's my opinion that the fever i[s]
only virulent among them during those years when the[y]
swarm—in fact—

". . . it's my opinion that it is the effect of the fever upon them which *makes* them swarm!"

In the sudden silence which fell, he added, again timid, "Wouldn't you agree?"

There was no time for much agreement or disagreement. All through the days the four-fold march went on and on; all through the nights myriad fires burned and glowed. Not since the continent had emerged, molten and hissing and steaming from the sea had the land seen such activity. The campfires and the watchfires blazed, the crybabies wailed as if heartbroken in the bush and forest. Beyond, inside the ever-concentrating rectangle, the rips could be heard, coughing and snarling uneasily.

Between twenty and fifty square miles was the ultimate area set by the over-plan for Phase Three. For quite some time before this compression was reached, however, the rips had been standing and fighting with increasing frequency. But the lines of men and rorks hemming them, pressing them in, were thicker now. The savage beasts were speared and clubbed, shot to death, torn apart by powerful claws. Men were, to be sure, sometimes wounded, and rorks as well. But prompt first and subsequent aid resulted in surprisingly and gratifyingly few fatalities.

Finally the ultimate area was reached, somewhat northeast of the continent's center. This was not quite convenient, in terms of the terrain and the over-plan; so it was, so to speak, rolled back. And then the third phase began in earnest.

A corridor was opened, about a mile wide; "troops" to line or to create it being withdrawn from the other flanks, which immediately proceeded to close in. The rips were driven out of the ultimate area and along the corridor. They were allowed no rest, no time to pause and make stands. Their pursuers worked in shifts, by lamplight and by torchlight and by the light of great blazing fires. By force of arms, by noise, by gunfire and pikethrust, by stones cast, the rips were forced down the corridor opened for them that led to the selected place on the Western coast.

Unmapped and unknown the greater part of that coast, like the interior, may have been. But this part of it, rimmed by sheer cliffs falling hundreds of feet into the troubled seas, this part of it had long been known and long avoided.

Its boiling and reef-infested waters bore the name of Kill-Man Gulf.

Every vessel that the Wild Tocks could muster—dugout, raft, catamaran—plied in a great arc where the waters of the gulf disembogued into the Western Sea. The single Station boat, making up in speed for its singularity, joined the picket line; and overhead, as close to the water as safety allowed, the skimmers supplied their armament to the blockade.

But few were the rips that survived long enough to be picked off.

The fourth and final phase of the campaign was made with less noise but equal thoroughness. The forces now deployed along the coasts looking for rip breeding grounds—sandy beaches, between high water mark and true ground. Had the creatures been live-breeders, the task might have been simpler—or might have been harder —but at any rate, different. However, they were oviparous monotremes of a sort, and by this time even a child was able to know what to look for: low, rounded, sandy mounds, heaped with sea wrack, the decomposition of which supplied warmth to aid the slow hatching of the eggs.

It was not necessary to destroy the leathery-looking clusters entirely. The blow of a hack, the thrust of a pike, or even a fire-sharpened stick or a spear of sort, improvised from a sharpened shell-shard was sufficient. The sea birds gorged themselves upon this unprecedented feast. But sometimes the searchers found the mounds already broached, the egg husks dry and scattered, and they knew that other predators had beaten them to it.

The last of the mopping-up was on the east central coast, and Ran was bringing his white flag down the sloping shelf rather late one afternoon when his ear-speaker gave a preliminary hum.

"Skimmer Five here—Ranny?"

"Starchy?"

"Seems to be a sort of cove or inlet about two leagues down from where you are. I doubt if it can be seen from shore in either direction . . . cliffs cut it off . . . but think I can see sand. I'm going in—in fact, I'm almost here—yes, sand—and put down and see if I can take care of it my—"

Ran broke in. "Be careful, Starch. There may be tricky updrafts there. Or down ones, for that—"

A rueful laugh. "You're telling *me*? Um—" A mutter.

Ran, mildly disturbed, said, "Hold off a bit, will you?" For answer there was only quick, troubled breathing. Then another voice—Harb's—broke in.

"Pull out of there, Motor Aide. Right now. Do you—?"

Brief; brief and terrible, was the sound of the crash in their ears. From down the coast a single gust of flame shot up into the air. Then came the smoke. Then silence.

Finally, after a long moment, Harb murmured, " 'Fear no more the heat of the sun . . .' "

But Ran had something else in mind. "Or the Q Ship," he said.

CHAPTER NINE

Manton's death was not made to seem vain by an absence of rip egg nests; the nests were there, all right, and if he had not observed the inlet possibly no one else would have. This put Ran to thinking about something, and he found out rather soon that others were thinking of it, too.

Norna, for one.

It had been some days since he had seen her, exactly how many, he couldn't remember; and now, looking at her, he seemed to see some reflection of how he himself must look. She was thinner, wearied, eyes reddened, not overly clean, hair tangled and in places white with dried salt spray. Sand clung to her feet and ankles; she scraped them on the sparse grass.

"I'm thinking of Flinders," she said, abruptly.

"You are!" He looked at her, sharply. "Curious. . . . Well, I've just been thinking of him myself."

She nodded. The sun was warm, the air clean and smelling of the sea and the little marshy estuary not far away, and of the tiny yellow flowers now suddenly out in great profusion. Down a ways on the shore a Tame Tock suddenly picked up a ruined egg cluster and tossed it, smack, at a rork. For a moment Ran tensed. But before he could move or speak, the rork had whirled around and, with a great backward movement of a powerful foot and leg, splattered the man with mud. The Tock stood there, foolish and gaping. His fellows hooted and snorted at him. The rork made a sound which might have been meant for laughter. Ran relaxed.

"Yes . . . I means, not just the Mister and all that . . . how he's a danger . . . But we's not been into his country. If rips be's there—"

She had put her finger on it. If any rips remained in or around the Crag—and, probably, some did—then they might eventually reconstitute their former numbers. There was, he mused, uncertainly, some belief that a species could never make a come back if its numbers were reduced beyond a certain point; other factors than mere sexual coupling being involved. If this were true or not he did not know, nor did he know what the number might be. Possibly, probably, it might well differ from species to species.

But if enough rips did remain about Flinders Crag then the whole ardous campaign would have gone for nought.

"What do you think, Norna?" he asked. And she told him.

They found Tan Carlo Harb sitting under an improvised lean-to overlooking the Eastern Sea. He was more like his old self, now that the campaign was almost over. He greeted them with a flap of his hand. "Pull up a tree stump . . . or something," he invited. "Or just squat, if you want to be picturesque and barbaric and all that. I've had enough sand in my crotch, thank you. *Well.* I can offer you cold drinks once again, and I shall insist upon your taking them before you oblige me to listen to whatever it is that I can tell you are just bursting to confide in me."

He beamed, cheerfully. "I must say that I feel at least ten years younger. The trouble is, I am not *quite* sure that I *wish* to. Ah, the drinks. Hmm, yes, we shall need a new toast, shan't we? How tiresome." He lifted his glass.

"Dead rips," he gave them.

They returned it. "Dead rips!" Ran had clear forgotten

how incredibly good a long, cold drink could feel. He seemed to feel this one all the way down.

The SO frowned very slightly. "Now, let me see, before you two young things begin burbling and babbling, now, what was it that I wished to speak about . . . ? Oh, yes. That nasty old rat, Flinders. . . . Dear me, what have I *said*?"

Feeling slightly foolish, Ran muttered, "Well, that's what we wanted to remind you about."

"*Re*mind me? Why, do you suppose that I have for*got*ten it? For one moment? Never-a-bit. No. Flinders must come to heel. Flinders must police his area. To begin with, realizing full well that he thinks that *he* has cause to hate *me* (which he certainly *does*; ho ho ha), I intend to turn the tables and non-plus him a bit. That always puts savages off balance. So. I am going to issue him an amnesty—issue? Grant. I'm granting him amnesty. Then, while he is still slobbering and wondering what he should think about *that,* I am going to get him to de-rip his pesky little country. Like me to tell you how?"

The plan of Tan Carlo Harb was this: The Mister Flinders was to be asked to duplicate the campaign against the rips, under supervision nominally and tactfully described as assistance. For this, he would be paid a sum of money in chits redeemable, not merely at the Station's Tocky Store, but in the store where Guildsmen traded. Flinders would be furnished transportation there and back, and he could use the chits to buy anything at all that was for sale; or he could establish credit.

"I will probably extend this privilege to everyone, eventually," said Harb, contentedly. "After all, they keep shipping the stuff in, you know, and there are buildings and buildings oh just *jammed* with it. Everyone. Wild Tocks, Tame Tocks, those wonderful uncivilized people whom the rorks have been keeping as pets—yes, why not? Rorks, too. Although what *they* could *want* to buy is beyond me. I mean, they haven't even any necks to string *beads* around! Anklets, maybe. *Well*. But Flinders gets the first crack at it, don't you see, to entice him to be nice.

"But I'm not going to allow him a flat fee. I want him to have his heart in this, I want him to think of killing rips every single minute. So I'm giving him a bounty. So much per head or tail or pair of ears. Cash on delivery. What think you?"

Ran and Norna looked at each other. Without a word, they nodded. Harb waved his hand. "Over to you, then, cute. Take care of the details. I intend henceforth simply to sit here until my poor tired feet put out weeny *tendrils*. Go, my children. Go. Go. Go."

Ran arranged the matter from his command post. Reldon, the Commercial Aide, was as red-eyed as most of them, but the redness was no longer from drinking, and his hands didn't tremble anymore. The matter of heading a truce team, or whatever it might be called, and finishing up the war on rips in Flinders Country, was perhaps not obviously under his jurisdiction as Commercial Aide. But it fitted under it without difficulty; and besides, he had never been in South Tockland, and was eager to seize the chance to go. Ran had some idea that the man was not too eager to return to the Guild Station, anyway— to the same dreary, useless routine; to the waiting bottle and the bottles of waiting friends. Perhaps it might not be a bad idea to post him in Wild Tockland for permanent duty.

Reldon, then, headed the truce team. There were Tame and Wild Tocks on it, and a few rorksmen; these last having shown a perception of terrain and ecology which bordered on the extra-sensory. It was not deemed advisable, though, or even particulary helpful, to include rorks.

The truce team was skimmered down southwards, and Ran, beginning to feel the inevitable letdown of the anticlimax, set about finishing up the work. There was one thing which he did want to see settled. The powwow had only established a one year's peace between men and rorks. Ran declared that at the end of the year a second powwow would be held, to discuss the possibility of extending the peace. He found no opposition to such a meeting, though his expressions of personal feeling—"Of course a perpetual peace is possible! Haven't we just finished proving that?"—met with noncommittal reactions as often as not.

Finally, finally, the last inch of coast was pronounced cleared; the forces which had worked clear around the continent met, and closed the circle. There was a jubilation of sorts, but it lasted less time than expected. Everyone seemed suddenly to wake up and realize that they had other things, customary things, to do. Garden plots must be tended, fishing-craft repaired and nets mended, houseys to be reinforced against the damage of the rains.

Offices to be returned to.

One day the beach at Point Conclusion (as Ran named it) was crowded. The next day only a few were left. "Let's go for a swim, shall we?" he said to Norna. She could not swim, it developed, so he offered to give her a first lesson. Naked, here in open daylight, with others—though not many others—visible. No; Norna refused. Her single undergarment, though, was not bulky enough to impede her arms and legs, and she proved an apt enough pupil.

"Well, that's enough for now, I guess," he said, presently. She stood up as he released her, and the sudden sight of the sodden garment clinging to the form of her young body sent his feelings flying. She understood immediately, and flushed; but then her eyes turned to the shore.

"That grove of trees over there. . . ." he murmured in her ear. Arm in arm they waded ashore, first the shore and then the woods seeming a hundred leagues away. For only an instant it seemed that the cloth resisted his fingers, clinging stubbornly to her skin. And then it came away and there was nothing between them but the beating and pounding of their hearts.

Pia Sol had half completed its long march down the sky when they emerged from the woods and walked towards the skimmer which served as command post. An insect buzzed somewhere, louder and more insistently. So great was his preoccupation that not until he had come directly abreast of the skimmer did he realize that he was hearing no insect but a signal buzz.

He leaped into the craft and pressed the cam. "Skimmer Sixteen here. What—"

Harb's voice, high and vicious, shrilled in his ear. "Where in the Hell have you been off to?" it demanded. "I've been trying to reach you for—"

"I was out swimming," Ran said, a sullen note in his voice.

"Swimming! Yes, I'm sure you were. And diving, too, I have no doubt. Well, listen, stud—" Suddenly the SO's voice broke. He resumed again, a moment later, in a dull, quiet tone. "Sorry. Sorry. Don't mind me. Listen . . . You don't know what's been happening down South, do you? It's my fault. All my fault. I should have known better. Oh, I should have known. . . ."

One of the Wild Tocks had thrown himself over the edge of the Crag. Miraculously, he had lived, and although it was obvious he could not live for long, he had managed to tell enough of what had happened before he died.

Even in the warmth of latest summer blending into earliest autumn, Flinders Country looked bleak and gaunt. The grass had a pinched look about it. Ran looked from the faces which looked grimly at him, looked around the landscape. It seemed to be familiar—recognition suddenly snapped his eyes clear. He and Norna had passed this way as Flinders' captives. Something . . . something just about here had arrested his attention.

"The cairn," he said.

Jun Mallardy nodded. His eyes were bloodshot, his upper lip seemed frozen into a snarl. "Shows ye the cairn," he said. It was not far off. The skull that had been there in Cold Time was still there now. Only no snow mantled it now; instead, there was reddish moss—

It was not moss. It was hair.

And it was not yet a skull. It was a head.

"Reldon!"

"Be's that's his name?" Mallardy nodded, almost indifferently. "A many names. All's dead."

The eyes looked right at Ran. The mouth seemed trying to say something to him. Ran's hands gripped each other. So near, Reldon had been, so near to climbing up forever from the pit of hopelessness that had wasted his years. *Neither here nor there nor up nor down is there anything that's any better* . . . He was trying to say something—

Dead rorks? Dead rips? *Dead Flinders!*

"Flinders did it," someone said. "Flinders did it, Flinders did it, Flin—"

A hand dug into Ran's shoulder, shook him. Abruptly the voice ceased. He recognized it now. Edran Lomar's voice. Jun Mallardy was speaking now. "Flinders did it says. Yes. Asks, 'But why?' I gots no answer. My brothe Sai gone up there, and Tig Owelly, and—You knowsn' their names. We does. Be's sure, their heads hangs up there on the Crag. 'Why?' May's be the poguey old Mis

136

ter saw's chance to gets back for all's feuds, olds and news. May's be's he just can't stand the thought of peace...."

"Never matter, why. Flinders wants blood."

The other growled and snarled like a rip. "And we s'll gives him blood. He s'll haves blood enough to swims in. And—" he swung around, thrusting his face into Ran's, "—Guildsman! Be's sure! He s'll have blood enough to *drown* in!"

All the other clans were there. If shouts could raze rocks, the cry that went up then would have shattered Flinders Crag into rubble . . . into dust.

The massacre of the truce team, which had trustingly entered into the Camp after its Mister's acceptance of amnesty and terms, had been a mad act. Fenced into his rocky, reeking little country, the opportunity to live at peace had let no light into his hot and festering mind. He operated on a level so low that Harb's hopeful vision had passed right over without Flinders seeing it. Flinders was able to understand one thing only: all not of his kith and clan were his enemies: here were enemies ready to place themselves in his house and hands! Agree? He would have agreed to fish for the sun at the bottom of the sea, if such agreement would have lured them in.

And now all his people had fled up into the Crag-girt camp, and the Crag was beleaguered. In a sense, the war on the rips had been forgotten, swallowed up into the war on Flinders. Nevertheless, what remained to do in the former fitted in well with the latter. The be-siegers formed a circle and gradually closed in. No doubt the few rips found suffered death as much as proxies for Flinders as for their own sakes. But then things reached a stalemate. Those above could not come down; those below could not go up, for the single narrow path and its approaches were guarded by day and by night. True, (Ran reflected), discipline and its sustentation were not within the power of the Wild men for long. Flinders's guard might relax . . . eventually. But, so . . . even-tually . . . might the siege.

And then it would be all to do over again: Rips, Flinders, feuds, fever. . . . Was this land never to have rest? He himself was the catalyst which had brought about all the recent and present action and reaction. It was up to him to resolve it all.

137

The skimmer—in the careful days of poor Starchy Manton—was considered fit to take five men. Ran packed it with fifteen, selecting the lightest ones he could find. It would take about two Wild Tocks to equal one well-nourished Guildsman in weight, anyway, he reflected. When it was well dark . . . that was the time.

He waited for seemingly endless hours. Then the distant night burst into noise and light. A band of 'locksmen, holding their matches glow-end down under the cover of cloaks improvised from such spare dresses as the women could hastily round up, crept close enough to the point known to hold the guards on the path—and opened fire. The distance and angle and darkness were such that it was not likely anyone could hit anyone else. Ran did not care about that. All that he wanted was noise.

And under its cover he skimmed down into the farthest, darkest corner of the Camp, and deposited his men. Twice more he made the trip. And then those within attacked. Common sense and ordinary discipline should have restrained those of Flinders' men down below to remain at their guard posts, but neither quality was abundant among them. When the shooting and shouting began above them they abandoned their position at once, and headed to defend their homes. And at this, all those below came streaming, scrabbling, climbing, crawling up the path.

They found the gate already half open for them. The fight had begun in the darkness, but it ended in light enough. It was by the blaze of his own blazing camp that they cornered Flinders. They tied his hands and feet and threw the rope over a beam. He swung there, upside down, screaming obscene imprecations while they carefully placed a small keg beneath his head. Then they cut his throat and lowered him a foot or two.

He died as Jun had promised. He drowned in his own blood.

CHAPTER TEN

Some day, Ran thought to himself, a great road would run through Rorkland, joining the North and the South.

It was fortunate, ironically enough, that the present turn of events had begun when it did—when the human race was still tired. He tried to envision what that road would be like, and to calculate how near it would pass to the Plain of Lights.

The Plain of Lights! What glory! And he and Norna— Norna had left him again, this time over Lindel. She had suggested he might care to chose, he had angrily refused. But leaving was her own idea entirely. Just as well. She had a wild sweetness to her, and a wild tartness, like some unhusbanded tree of the forest and its small, shy fruits. This what he had wanted when he came here. To get away from the past, from things pruned and cultivated, to tread the untroubled soil of the naked landscape. And he had gotten his wish and heart's desire, gotten full and heaping measure of it.

He did not begrudge a moment of it all. But he had no intention of plunging headlong down a cliff.

"After all," he said to Lindel, "you're scarcely the most demure, tamed little creature that ever was." She smiled. "You were raised here, you go your own damned way . . . in fact, you're a rather wild little poppet, yourself. And a rather hot little one." But she was civlized, too. Norna wasn't, despite the veneer of civilization gained from her father. Norna could read—just about. She knew a song or two. Her faint glimmerings of history, science, culture, the whole galactic world, were just that. Glimmerings. No—

Ran had had enough of wildness, nature, and the children of nature—barbaric chieftains and maidens. He would do his job, as he had been doing it; do it damned well, too. And then, one way or the other, he would depart. There were other worlds to see, on which the yoke of the Guild System rested lightly, if at all. The so-called "Free Worlds," for example.

But there was time enough for that. The Q Ship was still a long time from the day when he would stuff her astonished holds with redwing. And, meanwhile—

Meanwhile the cycle of the sun had rolled around again. It was the time of the second great powwow. Once again the rolling meadows around Hollow Rock were dotted with the figures of men and of rorks. Tan Carlo Harb spoke to them from his platform outside the pavilion.

139

"Why should there not be lasting peace?" he asked "The differences between men and rorks were not greate than those between men and other men. The Wild peopl did not trust the Guildsmen and the Guildsmen did no trust the Wild people. And between the Wild peopl themselves—was not there not always war, and war?"

A murmur arose when he paused. Whether of agree ment of otherwise, was hard to say. And in the pause slowly, old Dominis arose from the rock on which he'. been sitting. His beard was no whiter, certainly, but hi voice was a bit weaker.

"Peace, says. And war. I sees the small ones, now nots the same as times was. They s'll all grows up, says Fever s'll not kills 'em. Nor feudsing. A year ago, be' I couldn't thinks so. Be's that I hates a Guildsman ' much 's a rork. Now, says, I gots no hates for neither.' He sat down, rather abruptly.

A pity, Ran reflected, that the old man couldn't have developed that line more. But then someone else aros to speak, interrupting his regretful thoughts.

It was one of the minor Misters, a chief named Tarmi Ran scarcely knew him. He had a rather reedy voice, on had to strain to listen to him.

"—no more fever, says. Thinks that be's a good thing May's be right. I s'll not says, be's bad. But I says thinks on this—if men won't be's dying of fever, rork won't be's dying of fever, either. Ah, says? Means mor men, more men, more men. Means, more rorks, too, don'ts it? More rorks, more rorks. . . ."

He was getting to them. It took time for him to de velop his thoughts, they dealt with unfamiliar conceptions. But he was getting to them.

"Now. What be's it that men wants? Redwing, be'sn' it? Redwing, says. Pulls it, chops it, trades it, cures it. Redwing. So. What be's it that *rorks* wants—Ah?"

The background murmur rose. He was *definitely* getting to them. People moved restlessly, spoke to their neighbors. The rorks, for the most part reclining, folded between their legs, made neither sound nor movement. And the rorkmen leaned upon their staves (they had brought no clubs this time—or, if they had, had left them somewhere out of sight of the powwow) and smiled their strange, impassive smiles. The smell of woodsmoke came strong to Lomar's nose, and, faintly, the smell of redwing.

"Ahhh . . . Rorks haves to eats, same as everythings. And, says, what's it be's that rorks eats? Says?"

Someone in the crowd cried out the answer. A dozen voices took it up, a score, a hundred.

"Redwing! Redwing! Redwing!"

Nodding and nodding, the Mister Tarmi waited for them to be done. "Redwing, says. Right. Now. I akses. Don't says, Tarmi be's talking against peace. No. I just akses. If men wants redwing and if rorks wants redwing, and if there be's *more* men and *more* rorks, why—sees?— may's be soon, may's be later, comes the times when a man goes to chops a stalk of redwing, says, I wants this. And comes a rork, and says—ahhh—*I* wants this."

And he sat down among tumult.

Ran raised his hands for silence and waited patiently until he got it. "There's a Guildsman who has something to say."

It was the Second Aide, Lindel's father, Aquilas Arlan, so nervous, and yet, obviously so sure, that he quite forgot to titter.

"The only sensible answer to this question," he said, "is to partition the land." There was silence. "Divide it up," he explained. "So that—"

Jun Mallardy leaped forward. "Who be's to draws the lines?" he cried.

"Why—naturally—the Guild—"

He was drowned out by the clamor of voices. Ran looked at Harb. Harb nodded. Ran looked over towards the rorks and their men. Still none of them had moved. He caught the eye of the one called Tranakh. And Tranakh, his smile as bland (if bland it was) and curious as ever, made the slightest of movements. Gradually, gradually, the noise died down. There were still those who wanted to speak, but Ran met no one's eye. Harb met no one's eye. They seemed to be waiting for something. Gradually the quiet grew into absolute silence.

Still no one spoke.

Then, from among the ranks of the as yet unspeaking, a huge old rork unfolded its legs and got up. Slowly it advanced towards the men, slowly, steadily, closer than any rork had yet come that day. It had something in its mouth. The crowd fell back from either side. It was not

so much uneasy, not so much astonished, as waiting
And still the great creature went on.

And stopped perhaps five paces from Tarmi.

It lifted one foot and removed what it had been holding
in its mouth, and, with that foot, so curiously like and
yet so vastly unlike a longer, more dangerous human
hand, it lifted the thing up slowly, that all might see
what it was.

A redwing plant, fresh-pulled, by the looks of it. Slowly, but with effective blows, it beat the root-end of the
stalk against the ground till the clods of earth were
loosed from it. Slowly, as all looked on in wonder, crowding closer, it broke the plant into two pieces. And slowly
it ate the stalk piece.

And then, still slowly, it offered the leaf piece to Tarmi.

The solution, then, was so obvious, that it had until
then been missed. Men and rorks had no need to com-
pete for redwing, now or ever, no matter what their
numbers might be, for *each species used a different part
of the plant!*

Talk went on, of course, by sheer momentum, but
everything had really been settled in that few minutes of
slow pantomime. And when it was at last and at length
agreed that men would pull up no plants of redwing in
Rorkland, but would instead go to gather the leaves
which the rorks would leave behind for them, it seemed
a wonder that this had not been clearly understood from
the very start.

"Well, I'm very pleased," Harb said, slowly. "I'm really
very pleased. It all seems so neat that I keep thinking
there must be some catch to it."

"There are probably a million catches," Ran said.
"Sometimes they're called by fancier names—'challenges,'
for example. We'll face them when we come to them."

The SO nodded, not quite convinced. "I can see one
right now, before we even come to it. Surely the demand
for redwing is not infinite. Not in the kind of frozen condition things are now, and have been for so long. Suppose
the Rocks expand and increase and learn all kinds of
needs and wants? They won't be satisfied with old clothes
and hack blades and sulphur forever, you know. What
happens when they go on wanting to increase the market
and the market isn't going to increase?"

"That's a long, long way from now," Ran said. Harb brightened.

"Yes, it is. Of course it is. *I* won't have to deal with it. I shall be eating lotos or something on a simpler and more complicated planet, nice old Harb, he spins such interesting yarns, eh? When I'm retired."

Thus, his reaction to it all. Ran wasn't sure yet what his own would be, or even should be. But Lindel was. "They *will* move you," she told him. "There just isn't any doubt about it."

"Eh?" He looked at her, fondly, slightly bemused. His wild colonial girl! "Who? Move me where?"

"The Guild Directorate!" She seemed slightly impatient. "I know that they'll confirm your provisional rating. You'll be moved from three to seven. It's inevitable, because you've got a record, now. They handed you an impossible assignment, and yet you did it. You can really have any place you want after this, you know. Seven! Which would you like best? Hercules, or Tarquin? Or Transfer Ten?"

"Well—"

She babbled on, happier than he had ever seen her. "Is this what you want, really?" he asked, at last.

She broke off and looked at him in absolute astonishment. "Why, of course. It's what I've always wanted— all I've ever wanted. To get away from here and out where things are *alive*! Civilized! A decent life, oh, Ranny!"

And he realized that it was true, and all she ever did want, really—marriage to someone of a higher Guild rank, and a soft and safe comfortable career—everything according to the book. "We might even go back to Old Earth," she was saying. "You've got family and they have connections, naturally. Why, we could have an apartment in Rocky Mountain Complex. . . . In a few years you could be a ten!"

All she ever wanted. And all that he did not want. Too bad. Too bad for Lindel, anyway. Too bad, Lindel. The road through Rorkland would mean nothing to her, nor any of his own dreams. Because these dreams would now start coming true.

With men and men and men and rorks at peace, with the crippling fever wiped out, the continent could now start the work of building a new and decent life from

143

its own resources. The people would not need to remain any longer a gang of errand boys for a fossilized oligarchy a world of light-years away. They had much to learn from the rorks, had barely begun to suspect how much, but the rorks might prove apt pupils, too. It was so very lucky that all this was happening now, *now*, with the rest of the human race still tired and frozen in its stodgy ways. No danger, this way, of the Tocks and rorks being overwhelmed by an exploitive technology from outside. They could go at their own pace until, eventually, they would outpace the others.

And Ran? What did *he* want? He knew, now. He wanted this. No other planet, no other world. Here was home and here he would stay and help. Only—

Only something seemed missing. Someone.

Norna.

He would find her, though. And tell her that he had made his choice.